SECRETS
DIVIDE

Dee –
I hope
you enjoy
reading
my book
Julie Metros

JULIE METROS

DEDICATION

To my family
My son, Daniel,
My mother
My siblings, Jim, Tom, Patti, Barb, Clare and Jack,
My stepchildren, Christopher and Jill,
And always, in memory of my dad.

DISCLAIMER

Although inspired by a true event, this book is a work of fiction. Any reference to real people, events, businesses, organizations or locales are intended only to give the fiction a sense of reality and authenticity. The characters, their conversations, and conflicts are products of the author's imagination and used fictitiously. The names of all involved changed to protect their descendants. Any resemblance to actual people, living or dead is entirely coincidental.

ACKNOWLEDGMENTS

I would like to express my gratitude to my family and friends who saw me through this book; who supported me, shared their comments, and had faith in my abilities by pre-ordering my book, especially:

Linda Dutkiewicz, my alpha reader and friend, for her feedback, her encouraging words, and keeping me sane while waiting for reviews.

My beta readers, Katie Battani, Rita Bentzinger, Christy Johnston, Steve McDonald and Mary Jo Ward. I appreciated your feedback.

Nancy Luckow for loaning me her grandfather, Eugene N. Hastie's books, High Points Of Iowa History and Hastie's History Of Dallas county for research.

CHAPTER 1

April 13, 1903

Deep in her thoughts, Claire Johansson sat alone at the kitchen table with her hands cupped around her teacup. She lifted the cup to her mouth and took a sip, "Ugh!" she said aloud. Her tea now lukewarm.

Just a year ago, I had a houseful of children; she thought. She knew what day it was. April 13th. The day that changed their lives forever. That Sunday night, a brutal murder took her two youngest children away from her. For the first time in her life, Claire felt unneeded and lonely. As far as she recalled, she always took care of someone or something. As a young girl, she helped her mother care for her grandparents and with the household chores. Her older brothers died from influenza leaving just a twelve-year-old Claire to help her father with the farm chores. Claire continued to milk the cows, feed the chickens, and help with repairs around the farm until her father finally hired a farmhand to help.

Lukas worked at the farm shortly after emigrating from

Sweden. Unable to speak a word of English, Claire tutored the blonde blue-eyed Swede in the evenings. A mutual admiration developed, and Lukas knew what he needed to do. He learned the words to request permission from her father to court his only daughter. Claire continued to tutor Lukas and a year later when they married, he was almost fluent at speaking English. Lukas still struggled with the W sound and the letter "v" replaced it. When excited or angry, his rants became an unusual blending of English and Swedish. After they married, she relinquished her milking duties and took over the household chores. Her days spent tending to the vegetable garden, churning butter, preparing meals and endless sewing. When a bout with tuberculosis left her father too weak to work on the farm, she found herself back in the dairy barn milking the cows side by side with her husband. Eventually, their children were born, and it forced Lukas to hire a farm hand.

Now, with all the children out of the house, Claire found her days idle. With just the two at home, the time spent gardening, laundering, and mending lessened. After years of preparing meals for nine people, Claire found it difficult to cut back on her recipes and still made too much food. Despite his feeble attempt to say no, Jacob graciously accepted her baskets filled with a warm dinner or rolls for breakfast. That's the least she could do. Jacob owned his farm next to theirs but continued to milk their cows twice a day. Claire even convinced him to drop off his dirty clothes for her to wash. She hoped and prayed he would marry soon. Boys never learned domestic skills, she thought.

Like a good wife, Claire continued to care for her husband, but he no longer appreciated it. He hardly spoke to her; and even then, it was only one or two words. He would disappear for hours each day and retire soon after his evening meal.

Claire tried to keep herself busy. She knitted or crocheted booties and blankets for their ever-growing family. Her sewing basket overflowed with clothing embroidered and sewed for her unborn grandchildren. The fruits and vegetables she canned shared with her children and neighbors. News of an ailing neighbor or mother in labor sent Claire immediately to their home to help out. Once a week, she joined neighboring women for afternoon tea. She met with the women's guild at their church. Her church. No one went with her. She quietly sat in the back pew immersed in prayer. Prayers for her broken family.

But with all that, she found herself alone for hours each day. Alone with her memories of happier days from long ago and the recent sad days. Claire prayed whenever her thoughts turned to sadness.

Now that spring had arrived, Claire hoped her days would be busier. The last winter frost would be over soon, and she could work in the garden. The long frigid, snowy winter kept her imprisoned in her own home. That morning she rose to a bright sunrise. She quickly flung open curtains and windows to brighten up the rooms and chase away the winter blues. With the windows open, she listened to the refreshing sounds of spring, birds chirping, cows mooing in the pastures, pigs squealing in the mud, or the galloping sounds of a passing wagon on Poor Farm Road.

Claire felt the warmth from the spring breeze; bringing with it the pungent scent from the manure spread over the fields. Even after spending her entire life on a farm, the odor still caused her to wrinkle her nose. She thought about closing the windows facing the fields, but it had been a long winter filled with sadness and loneliness; she welcomed the fresh air, regardless of the foul odor.

Bang-bang! The sound of nearby gunfire startled her.

"Oh! That sounded close!"

Someone must have found a fox in their chicken coop, she thought to herself.

Gunfire never bothered her before, but with her home eerily quiet now, every sound echoed throughout the house and rattled the walls.

Just a year ago, she repeated her earlier thought. Her house full of laughter and sibling squabbles. One by one, her children left the nest to begin their own lives. Above her, the upstairs' bedrooms remained empty. Jacob now the only one she saw every day. Sitting by the window, she waited for him to wash up at their water pump. She quickly ran to the back door to wave him over to give him his laundered clothing or a warm meal. Sometimes, he would sit down for a quick meal; but most of the time, he graciously thanked her with a kiss on the cheek. She tried to engage him into conversation, but he hurried home to wash up. He recently started courting Isabelle, a young woman from church and he didn't want to show up late.

At afternoon tea last week, Eliza Davis suggested she take in boarders. Claire loved that idea and made a mental note to talk to Lukas later. It was foolish to let the two rooms stay vacant. Not to mention, it would give her something to do.

Lukas. *How can I talk to him when he won't answer me?* Her husband blamed her for his son's death. She didn't think he would ever forgive her.

Suddenly, Claire felt a pain in her chest. She placed her hand over her heart. A premonition. Someone was hurting. But who? Lukas? One of her children? Her grandchild? Jacob? She wasn't sure.

She worried about Lukas every day for the past year. Timmy's death hit him hard. He retreated into his own world; going through the motions but not understanding anything. She seriously doubted he remembers the girls' weddings, that more grandchildren were coming or that Gracie also died that night. The caretaker from the cemetery stopped by a few months ago following Lukas' recent visit during a blizzard. He expressed his concerns and worries that Lukas would freeze to death. He told Claire that Lukas visited the gravesite three or four times a week. Regardless of the weather; he knelt on the grass, mud or snow and cried for hours.

Even married and expecting, Anna Belle and Chloe would always be her little girls; she prayed they both delivered healthy babies with no complications. Anna Belle's baby due first and Chloe's, just a few months later. The stress of the trial and acquittal of Tom Landers could cause a premature delivery, but she worried in vain. Her daughters' healthy and happy as their babies grew inside.

"I think I will visit Anna Belle and Chloe tomorrow. I need to pick up a few things from the dry goods store," she said aloud. With both daughters living close to the shops, it gave her a perfect opportunity for Claire to visit.

John and Emma's growing family reminded of her own difficulties with childbirth. Just barely six months old, Baby Timmy would soon be a big brother. Emma's first pregnancy proved difficult; the baby took over her tiny frame forcing her to spend the last few weeks in bed. Chloe stayed with them but now she was married, there was no one to help. Timmy could be a handful, but she raised John to be a caring husband and father, he would help Emma whenever he could.

"I could visit John, Emma and baby Timmy too." Tomorrow, I will ask Jacob to hitch the wagon.

Lillian's health and well-being caused her sleepless nights. On her rare visits home, Claire could see that the daily nursing classes and overnight shifts at the hospital exhausted her. She looked tired but happy. Nursing was her calling. Lillian would say, "Mama, don't fret!" But that wouldn't stop Claire from worrying she would become ill or catch a deadly disease.

Shortly after she started nursing school, Lillian met Ben, a medical student in his final year. Their friendship eventually grew to a courtship. A secret courtship. The school forbade nursing students to date or marry, and violators expelled from school. Their close friend kept their secret. Lillian believed the head nurse knew but turned a blind eye. But they stayed diligent in hiding their romance; even visits to the Johansson farm carefully planned out. Both leaving the hospital at separate times and in different directions, then meeting up just a few blocks away.

And then there was Jacob. The rift between Jacob and Lukas, often, her primary reason for her extra church visits. Many an afternoon, she knelt alone in the church and asked God to heal their hearts. But it only got worse. The animosity for each other grew more with every passing day. She had prayed that living separately would help, but it still wasn't better. Jacob avoided Lukas.

Clip-clop. Clip-clop. The rhythmic sound of hooves hitting the gravel road outside interrupted Claire's thoughts.

An overwhelming uneasiness engulfed Claire. Lukas or one of her children needed her, and she didn't know which one.

* * * * * * * * *

Just a few blocks east, Anna Belle stood in the corner of the modest kitchen. She looked around the room from the large black stove to the basin sink and counter to the wooden hutch built by her sister's husband. In the center, a large kitchen table with two long benches ready for a large family. At each end, matching chairs. Seating for ten! If our family is as big as that table, there won't be room for any furniture, she thought.

Anna Belle turned her attention back to the machine in front of her. The wooden barrel of the washing machine stood waist high. A long lever attached to the middle of the lid, by turning the lever the contents agitated and the clothes washed. Another lever moved the rollers. Wet clothes fed through the rollers that squeezed out the excess water. She absentmindedly turned the handle and watched the white shirt pass through the rollers.

A few weeks ago, Robert surprised her with the washing machine. At first, she didn't think it would be helpful, but it took just one day of laundry to realize she was wrong. No continuous rubbing of clothes on the washboard. Twisting and turning several times to remove the water; only to find that, once hung on the line, water dripped for hours before the sun would dry them. In the winter months, the lines took over the kitchen as they crisscrossed the room. The stove lit to shorten the drying time. Clothes rotated closer to the heat until they were all dry.

Anna Belle laughed to herself as her protruding stomach bumped the barrel when she removed the shirt from the rollers. She dropped it to the wooden basket at her feet. The basket, heavy from the damp clothes, proved difficult for the pregnant woman to carry outside. Unable to hold it much longer, she let go and it fell to the ground. Thud! The basket landed hard. Anna Belle lifted the top shirt, shook it, and hung on the line with the wooden clothespin. One by one, she repeated these steps until she had finished. In a few hours, the warmth of the sun would dry the clothes.

"Oh!" Anna Belle exclaimed. A slight twinge at the base of her stomach. She placed her hand under her protruding belly and held it there for a second until the pain subsided.

It's too soon, but I had better send a message to Nellie, just in case, she thought. Nellie, her midwife, lived just a few blocks away. And if I have any more. Robert and Mama! But only if there were more. Robert, her husband, worked at a downtown insurance company, and wouldn't be home for several hours. It was barely ten o'clock now.

* * * * * * * * *

A few miles away, Duke laid on the floor of the stable. Next to him, his master's head rested on the hay-covered ground. His dust covered hat just a few feet away. The blue eyes stared across the barn but saw nothing. His face a mixture of dirt and tears. The faithful dog licked his master's dirty face. An arm lay across Duke's body, but the hand didn't stroke the canine's fur. Instead, it lay motionless nestled into Duke's side.

CHAPTER 2

Chloe placed the last dish on the drainer. She removed the kitchen towel thrown over her shoulder to dry the dishes and placed them on the shelf above the large sink. She looked around the kitchen to see if she missed anything.

Chloe loved her new life. Mrs. Charles Carter! Chloe Carter! She had dreamed of marrying Charles since elementary school. Charles surprised her with the house just weeks before their wedding. At first, it disappointed her he decided without her, but now Chloe adored their little house. Anna Belle lived just a few blocks away and Mama still close enough to visit for an afternoon walk. Plus, it was close to the center of Highland Park, the shops, and trolley station. Their proximity to Highland Park also meant many visitors. Family and friends would stop by for a spot of tea or just to say hello on their way to or from the shops. Some days, Chloe would join them; other times, she sat envious as they showed her their purchases.

Chloe giggled to herself as she remembered her brother, John's, comments. "Who are you punishing? You or Chloe? You are too close to the shops! Better lock up your money or you'll be living at the Poor Farm!" he teased Charles knowing his sister's love for shopping.

Now six months later, it was home. For years, Chloe filled her hope chest with linens, blankets, and quilts. Its contents now arranged around the house. Embroidered towels hung from the bar by the kitchen sink, a beautifully stitched quilt across their bed and a crocheted blanket over the wooden rocking chair.

Chloe rinsed the washcloth before wiping the kitchen table and counters by the sink. Satisfied that the kitchen was sparkly clean, Chloe moved to the parlor to rest her swollen feet. She sat in the rocker. Another surprise from her husband. Charles's passion was woodworking. One would be hard-pressed to find a room in their house that didn't include Charles' handiwork. He made the kitchen table, their bed frame, bookshelves, side tables and the rocker she sat in.

On the weekends, he retreated to the small shed behind the house; he sawed, hammered, and sanded for hours. So, engrossed in his work, he forgot to stop for meals. Frequently, Chloe carried his supper or dinner to him in a small basket. She would sit down on a wooden box and admired his dedication. She could watch him work for hours. They talked about their future, dreams, and desires. He had mentioned a few times he wanted to open a furniture store in town. But as the provider for his wife and future children, he pushed that dream aside and continued to work at the factory. A steady paycheck more important. Word spread of the quality of his pieces and he earned extra money building one-of-a-kind furniture for others.

While Charles' passion was woodworking; Chloe's was needlepoint. Like her husband, Chloe would spend hours embroidering or crocheting a gift for a family member or close friend. Next to the rocker, a basket full of balls of yarn, knitting and crochet needles, and several unfinished projects. Chloe pulled out the tiny booties she started a few days ago. She lovingly placed her hand on her round belly. She giggled to herself as she thought; I believe I'm carrying a watermelon.

She felt her baby kick her hand. Just a few more months until I meet you, she thought. "Just a few more months," she repeated. Her baby kicked again. Once she rocked, the baby settled down.

Knock-knock-knock!

"Who could that be?" She asked herself. It was mid-morning and the shops would be open soon for the day. She wondered what friend or relative stood on the other side of the door.

Chloe placed the booties back into the basket. She carefully stood using her arms to push herself up. When she was upright and didn't risk falling back down, she walked to answer the door.

"It's a bit early for a visit, isn't it?" She asked her guest. "Please, please, come in. Can I make you a cup of tea?"

CHAPTER 3

Jacob sat in the paddy's back wagon. The gravel road made it difficult to stay seated and forced him to hold on to the wooden bench with both hands. A tiny opening in the back door gave a view of their journey. People stopped and stared as the wagon passed by. They whispered to each other and pointed with puzzled looks as they wondered about the passenger or passengers in the back. He knew in a few hours they would all know; the news would spread throughout Highland Park like a prairie fire.

Earlier, he looked out as they passed his family home; he placed his face into the palm of his hands and shook his head. *How could this happen to me*, he thought shaking his head back and forth. Why now? Everything had fallen in place. His life exactly as he wanted. His land plowed and ready for planting. Seed ordered from the local dealer. Even living close to his father, he no longer dealt with him daily. Jacob still milked the cows either in the morning or evening but with only six cows, it was a one-man job. Jacob and Daniel, the hired hand, took turns with the milking duties. His father stayed clear of the barn.

He worried how his family would react to his arrest. Everyone except his father. No, he feared what his father would do. He heard stories; prisoners lynched before they had their day in court. How the public took the law into their own hands. He feared his father would have no qualms in hanging him. Even providing the rope or slipping the noose around his neck.

He thought about Isabelle. In his father's absence, Jacob attended a Church bazaar with his mother. With winter approaching, attendance at church services or events would dwindle and some members wouldn't see each other until the spring thaw. The church hall filled with young women hoping to snag a suiter for the long months ahead. One by one, the young women and men paired off. Finally, Jacob garnered up the nerve to approach Isabelle's father. His aloof demeanor well known, but with no other offers, her father reluctantly gave Jacob permission to call on her. His reputation of being a hard worker a saving grace. As a bonus, Isabelle received his mother's nod of approval. She came from a good family, was well-mannered and would make a good wife. Most nights they sat in silence under the watchful eye of her father. On the rare occasions they walked by themselves but after discussing the weather or an upcoming Church event, conversation evaded them. He expected that eventually he would grow to love her. But would she stand by him? Would her father let him continue to court her? They had her reputation to protect; especially with three more daughters to marry off.

The wagon came to an abrupt stop. Not expecting it, Jacob jerked forward almost falling off the bench. He heard the unlatching of lock. Seconds later, the door opened, and daylight flooded in.

"Step out," the detective ordered.

Jacob made his way to the door and stepped out. He squinted as he looked around; he recognized the alley. It was the same alley he had driven down delivering to the creamery. But this time he wasn't going to the creamery. He stood behind the police station and the jail.

Placing his hand on Jacob's forearm, the detective led him to the back entrance. The police chief sprung ahead of them and unlocked the door.

Jacob entered the building; Detective Maloney never released his arm. Chief Morrow stopped briefly to grab a set of keys hanging from a large nail. He led the way to a closed door, the large ring dangled from his hand. He opened the door and descended the steps; the keys jingling as he moved.

Maloney removed his hand to allow Jacob to enter the stairwell. He followed Jacob closely down the steps.

At the bottom, Jacob stopped. Despite his rogue personality, he stayed a model citizen. The closest he had gotten to the police station was riding past the building on his way to the creamery or running errands.

The two cells sat side by side; a dinner bell hung between them. Only a few pieces of furniture in each cell; a three-foot wooden bench and a wooden cot with a wool blanket. A bucket in the corner served as a privy. Both cells were empty.

Morrow opened the door of one cell and motioned for Jacob to enter. The cell door slammed shut. Jacob turned as the police chief locked the door.

"Mr. Johansson, I charge you with murdering your brother and sister, is there anything you want to say?"

"Huh, I don't understand. How? Why?"

"We will be back later to talk to you about the charges. If you need anything, ring the bell. Officer O'Reilly can help you," Detective Maloney pointed to the bell that hung between the two cells.

Jacob watched as the two policemen disappeared up the steps.

He sat down on the bench, placed his face in his hands and thought about his life. Everything fell in place; his farm was striving; his house finished, and he was courting Isabelle. What now?

* * * * * * * * * *

Knock-knock-knock!

The rapping of the door announced a visitor. Using the apron tied around her waist, Claire dried her hands. Then, she untied the bow, and hung it on a hook by the door. She walked across the parlor to the front door.

Detective Maloney and Chief Morrow stood on the front stoop.

"G'morning, Ma'am. Is Lukas around?"

"Oh, he is not here," Claire thought to herself I haven't seen him all day. Claire recalled waking to find him still in bed. A rare occasion as he usually left long before she had awoken. Then added, "I know he planned to go into town for supplies, but after that, I'm not sure." In all honestly, she didn't know where he went that morning but given the time of the year, she expected he went to pick up supplies for planting season.

Claire leaned out the door and peered towards the northern acreage. "He could be in the fields. Or in the barn working on the plow."

"Thanks, Mrs. Johansson."

Claire nodded and closed the door. She wondered why they wanted to talk to Lukas and hoped they had good news to share with him.

Detective Maloney placed his hand against his forehead to shield his eyes from the bright sun. He scanned the horizon from east to west.

"I don't see Lukas in the fields. Wanna' check the barn?"

Morrow looked towards the barn, then added, "I don't see his wagon around either. He could still be in town."

The law men hopped in their wagon and left the farm. They came upon one of the Johansson's neighbors. He slowed down his wagon to greet them, so the officers did too.

"What are you doing in this part of town?"

"Stopped in to see the Johansson's; looking for Lukas. He's probably still in town."

"I don't think so. I saw him heading north a few hours ago. His wagon was full of seed. I slowed down to talk to him, but he seemed to be in a hurry."

"Hmmm...." Detective Maloney glanced back at the farm. "We didn't see him around."

The sound of galloping horses interrupted their conversation. The cemetery caretaker's wagon raced towards them. He yelled out, "Detective! Chief!" He sounded frantic.

"What's wrong?" Chief Morrow questioned when he reached them.

"I came to talk to Mrs. Johansson. I'm worried about her husband, Lukas. He was at the cemetery earlier today. He was so distraught, crying, laying on the grave, yelling out he would see his son soon. I'm afraid he might do something drastic!"

"We were just at the farm; he wasn't there," Maloney replied.

The police chief added, "But we didn't check the barns. Should we go back?"

"Yea. Let's go back and search the farm and buildings!"

Maloney quickly turned the wagon around and followed the neighbor and caretaker back to the Johansson farm. When they arrived at the farm, the four men jumped out of their wagons and crossed the gravel road to the plowed fields. They spread out and called out for Lukas.

Joe, the neighbor yelled out, "Lukas!! Lukas!"

Just silence.

"Where's Duke? He's usually by his side when he is on the farm. Let's call for his dog!" Joe cupped his hands around his mouth and called out, "Duke! Duuukkkkeee!"

He stopped to listen. Still nothing. The others joined him.

"Duke! Come here, boy!"

In distance, they heard a faint bark.

CHAPTER 4

Inside the house, Claire had aimlessly wandered from room to room, and eventually made her way upstairs. Her first stop the girls' bedroom. She glanced around the room. It appeared frozen in time. Exactly as it looked when her last daughter married six months ago. The four beds positioned against the walls. The finely stitched quilts tautly covered the feathered mattresses. A lone dresser sat between two beds; the beds her oldest daughters once occupied. The items on the dresser, an old oil lamp and a doll, covered with dust.

Gracie's doll. One of her daughters placed it there following her death. Gracie always put her against her pillow every morning after making her bed.

Claire walked to the dresser. The room would need a good cleaning before she could even consider boarders. She ran her fingers over the top and smiled to herself as her finger drew a line in the dust. It had been months since she had been in this room. The day Chloe married Charles. She had helped Chloe dress for her wedding, Claire curled her hair and carefully calmed her nerves. Giving her the same advice, she had given Anna Belle, she told her what to expect on her wedding night.

She picked up the doll. It, too, dusty from months of solitude. Claire wiped the dust off its porcelain face. The glass blue eyes stared up at Claire; its black wig, made of mohair, tied with a faded pink ribbon at the top of her hair. The white dress now yellowed from age. No one played with the doll anymore. No one combed her hair or washed her dress. Like Claire, discarded and useless.

Claire sat down on an empty bed and sighed. She held the doll on her lap and looked around. Just a good cleaning, she thought to herself. She ran her free hand over the quilt. The bedding would need a good washing. With a little work, it would be acceptable for any boarders.

"This room used to be filled with laughter." *Now it is quiet,* Claire thought as she stood up.

And across the hall, another equally empty room. "I should check the boys' room too."

Claire walked across the landing to the other room. She surveyed the room. Like the girls' bedroom, frozen in time. On the dresser, a water pitcher and basin. A wooden toy on the floor by one bed.

"Just a good cleaning in here too," Claire said. Suddenly, she heard faint cries from outside. She stood to look out the window and saw the four men walking through the field across the gravel road. She quickly left the room and ran downstairs to check it out.

"Hello!!!" Claire yelled as she ran out the door. Outside, she could make out their cries. "Why are they calling for Duke? Something must have happened to Lukas," she asked herself.

Detective Maloney heard Claire call out and turned to see her running across the field.

"Detective," she gasped out of breath from running.

As she got closer, she realized who the other two men were; their neighbor, Joe, and the cemetery caretaker. The caretaker had stopped to see her a few times over the past year. He witnessed Lukas' breakdowns at the gravesite and felt Claire needed to know.

"I'm sorry to bother you, Ma'am." The Police Chief said as he walked towards Claire. "We are just looking for Lukas. We heard he left Highland Park hours ago." He glanced over at the caretaker and slightly shook his head. He didn't want to alarm Claire. But it was too late. He saw the concern in her face.

Lukas. Why are they looking for Lukas in the fields?

Claire spoke but the faint sounds of a dog barking interrupted her.

"That's Duke!" Joe yelled.

"Where's it coming from?"

They listened for more barks.

"Duke, ol' boy, where are you?"

Woof-woof! They all turned toward the barks.

"Quick! It's coming from the stable!" Joe sprinted towards the barn. The other men followed him with Claire at their heels.

Chief Morrow turned around when they reached the stable. "You best stay here, Mrs. Johansson. Let us check it out first."

"What do you think happened? Is Lukas hurt? Please, tell me! I am his wife, I must know!"

"You check it out," he said to the other men. "I'll explain the situation to Mrs. Johansson."

The situation? Claire thought.

"But, Lukas," Claire said hesitantly.

"Please sit. Over here," the police chief urged.

Claire watched as the men disappeared inside the barn. The door closed behind them.

"Let's sit," the chief said. He placed his hand on Claire's elbow and directed her to bales of hay next to the wooden fence. Claire sat down on one bale while the Chief sat on the other.

"What is going on?" Claire asked again.

"The caretaker saw Lukas at the cemetery today. He said Lukas was deranged, talking to himself, yelling out, calling Timmy's name."

Claire nodded. She knew about his trips to the gravesite.

"Yes, he has done this, many times over the past year. Last winter, he about got frostbite after sitting on the frozen ground during a blizzard."

"This time it was different. He yelled out I will see you soon."

Claire's eyes welted with tears. She remembered the gunshot she heard earlier. Claire assumed a neighbor killed a critter, but she knew what day it was. Usually, Lukas left the house long before she rose but that morning, he laid in bed mumbling incoherently. Claire caught bits and pieces; mostly, she heard her dead son's name repeated. Timmy, Timmy. She made him breakfast that he barely touched. Then without a word, he stood up, grabbed his hat, and walked out of the house.

"He didn't…" she began until the Police Chief interrupted her.

"We don't know. That's why we are looking for him. Uh, there's more." Morrow continued, "We came today to tell Lukas that we arrested someone this morning."

"Oh?"

"Your son, Jacob."

"Jacob?" she repeated. Claire placed her face into her palms and cried. Her family had fallen apart.

Oh, Jacob. Jacob, what have I done?

CHAPTER 5

Catherine Landers finished washing the last table. She looked around the room to make sure she had missed none. The dining hall now empty but just fifteen minutes ago, young men and women filled the room. Their conversations lively as romances blossomed or test answers compared.

Catherine grabbed a broom and swept the floors. The kitchen help would mop the floor after they finished washing and drying the dishes. Catherine crossed the hall and left the room through the double doors. Next to the doors, an opening in the wall allowed the students to collect their lunch. The leftover trays stacked neatly off to one side.

Inside the kitchen, a young man washed the dishes and placed them on the drainer where a second man dried them and stacked them on the shelf below the open wall.

"The floors are ready for mopping now," she yelled over to the dishwashers. The one drying looked at her and nodded. Catherine removed her apron and used it to blot her face dry. By the door, her cape hung concealing her satchel underneath it. The other hooks empty as the cooks left after they served the last meal. Their daily shift began at dawn.

Catherine placed her cape over her shoulders before tying it at her neck. She unfastened her satchel and pulled out a smaller bag. Opening it, she peeked in and satisfied with its contents placed it back in her bag.

Once outside, she made her way towards Highland Park. The streets now bustling with afternoon shoppers. She nodded at a few ladies from church. In front of Hill's Feed and Grain store, several wagons parked; she watched farmers load large bags of seed or grain into their wagons. Across the road, a familiar red and white pole attached to the front of the barbershop. A large sign in the windows offered cut and shave for 25 cents. Under the large window, wooden chairs shanked a large barrel table; on top a checkers game for patrons as they waited for their turn. Catherine passed by a familiar man. John Johansson. She smiled and nodded. He tipped his hat, but he didn't smile. He looked worried. I wonder why; she thought. She prayed his young wife was in good health. At a church service, she heard she was expecting again; so soon after her last child. Within minutes, she stood at a familiar door. Just seven months ago, her first visit to hire an attorney for her son. William McNally, Esq painted on the sign above the door.

Her son, Tom considered himself lucky that he kept his job at the coal mine. His weekly wages split four ways; some to his mother to help with household expenses, a part saved for his future, a little for fun and the rest to pay off his legal fees. Tom gave his mom that share and once a week, she would drop it off after her shift at the college.

Catherine climbed to the landing and opened the door. Inside, the secretary typed a letter.

"Good afternoon, Catherine!" she said looking up.

"Good afternoon, Sara!" The two women became friends over the past seven months. "How are your children feeling? Are they over that nasty cough?" Catherine continued remembering their conversation from last week.

"Yes, they are healthy," she replied as she retrieved a leather-bound book from the lower drawer. She flipped through the pages until she found the one with "Thomas Landers" written at the top. Catherine removed the tiny bag from her satchel and withdrew the money.

"I really appreciate Mr. McNally allowing Tom to make payments."

Sara smiled as she took the cash from her. Each week Catherine said the same thing and Sara responded the same too.

"Mr. McNally appreciates that you make your payments each week." The door behind her opened, she whispered so only Catherine could hear, "Speak of the devil."

"Mrs. Landers, how wonderful to see you. I trust you are doing well." Mr. McNally stopped to greet her.

"Yes, I am. And you, may I ask?"

"I am doing well. Busier than ever!" His business booming since the trial; there wasn't a criminal or accused for miles who hadn't requested his legal services.

McNally turned towards his secretary and said, "I will stop for supper before my meeting downtown. I won't be back until late. You may leave when you finished those letters. Please place them on my desk and lock up when you leave."

Sara nodded as he turned and left closing the door behind him. Sara counted the money and wrote the amount in the ledger.

"Just a few more payments left. I won't see you anymore."

"I will still stop in to visit with you," Catherine said with a smile.

"I better leave too," Catherine said eyeing the pile of handwritten papers sitting on Sara's desk.

"Oh, yes. If I hurry, I might have time to stop off at the dry goods store before going home."

Catherine stepped outside and descended the steps. She turned to walk east towards her home and almost bumped into Mr. McNally who stood a few feet away.

"Mr. McNally, did you forget something?"

"No, I mean, yes, I forgot, I mean, I wanted to ask if you would be so kind as to join me for a bite to eat. I'm heading to Water's Restaurant."

Catherine thought for a minute. Her stomach growled. She hadn't eaten since breakfast earlier that morning.

"Why, yes, I will, Mr. McNally."

"After you." McNally held out his arm in the restaurant's direction.

Confused by the attorney's invitation, Catherine pondered for a reason. She hoped her weekly payments were enough and that he would not demand the balance they owed. Adelaide no longer attended school and along with her brother, Tom contributed to the household expenses. This allowed Catherine to supplement Tom's payment hoping to pay off the debt sooner.

Inside the restaurant, Mr. Watkins rushed to the front to greet them, "Good afternoon, Mrs. Landers, Mr. McNally. Will you be dining with us?"

"Yes, a table for two, please."

"Please right this way." Mr. Watkins turned around and walked towards the back-dining room.

Now past the dinner hour, the dining room mostly empty; a few tables, recently vacated with dirty dinnerware scattered on top. Catherine recognized two students seated at the corner table, their books opened in front of them, drinking coffee. The male student smiled sheepishly at Catherine; she wasn't sure who is companion was. A female student. She wondered if the corner table chosen for wooing or studying.

The owner led Catherine and the attorney to a table off to the side. McNally held her chair as she took her seat.

Mr. Watkins handed her a printed menu and said, "I would highly recommend our stew today. I'm sure there is enough left for both of you to have a bowl."

Mr. McNally replied, "Mrs. Landers?"

Catherine nodded and smiled.

"We will take two bowls of the stew, please."

"And something to drink?" the restaurant owner asked.

"Tea with honey, please," Catherine said.

"Make that two."

"Thank you," he replied as he raced back to the kitchen.

They sat in silence for a minute then both spoke at the same time.

"Business is good?" Catherine asked as McNally said, "How is Tom doing?"

Catherine giggled. McNally smiled saying, "You go first. You were saying?"

Catherine said, "I asked how business was. Is it good?"

"Very well. Tom's trial and acquittal resulted in several requests from many to be their trial lawyer. After years of bill collecting, I am now finding myself at the court house weekly."

"That is good?"

"Yes. And how is Tom doing? Your other children?"

"Tom is working hard. He is taking extra shifts to keep himself busy. He really did have a crush on Grace. Her death hurt him. I pray that he will find someone else to love. He is a good man. Hardworking and will provide a good life for a special lady."

Catherine continued, "Michael is courting a young lady. The daughter of a coal miner. Laura is expecting again. In the fall. Adelaide stopped going to school and is working at the restaurant north of the station now. She is, and has always been, smitten with Jacob Johansson."

"Oh, speaking of Jacob, they arrested him this morning for the murder of his younger brother and sister. Timmy and Grace. His brother, John stopped by my office earlier. He is looking for an attorney. I have more work than ever, so I recommended a good attorney downtown."

"Jacob? Oh, my, how Claire must be beside herself."

Catherine remembered how she felt when the police arrested Tom. She remembered how scared she was for her son. She knew Claire would share the same feelings.

Mr. Watkins interrupted her thoughts, "Your tea," said as he placed the cup and saucer in front of her. He placed a second cup in front of McNally.

"I will bring your stew out now," he said as he turned and walked away.

Catherine took a sip of her tea. The tea tasted delicious with just the right amount of honey.

"Mrs. Landers," McNally said. "I was wondering if I might."

"Piping hot stew!" Watkins said interrupting him. He placed the first bowl on the table for Catherine. He turned to the tray sitting on a nearby table and picked up a second bowl for the attorney. A basket of corn bread muffins placed between them.

Catherine reached for a muffin at the same time as McNally. Their fingers touched, and they looked at each other for a few seconds. Catherine smiled before removing her hand.

"You were saying?" she asked.

"Oh, yes. Mrs. Landers, I was wondering," he turned to see if Mr. Watkins would interrupt them again. "I was wondering," he repeated. "Wondering if I might call on you one day?"

"Why, Mr. McNally, I am flattered." It had been a long time since Catherine enjoyed the company of a male caller. As a widow with four young children to raise, she hadn't a single minute to herself. Now they had grown, her time had come.

"But."

"Oh, no, no but. I would very much enjoy your company, Mr. McNally."

"Please, call me William," the attorney said.

"William. And you may call me Catherine. When would you like to call?

"This Sunday afternoon, if it is not too soon. The Presbyterian church is having a bazaar. It would honor me if you allow me to escort you. Would that interest you?"

"Yes, I would like that, Mr., er, William."

"I will be at your house at noon."

"And I will pack us a picnic lunch."

"As much as I enjoyed your picnic lunches, the ladies' guild is serving a lunch for a small donation. You provided several meals during the trial and I never paid you for."

They finished their stew in silence. Mr. Watkins returned to clear the dirty dishes. "Can I interest you in a piece of apple pie?

Mrs. Watkins' apple pie won a blue ribbon at the State Fair last summer."

William glanced at Catherine with a questioning look.

"No, thank you. I must get home. I have clothes hung outside that surely will be dry now."

"And I must catch the trolley for downtown." William reached into his breast pocket and pulled out a leather wallet. He took out a few bills, handed it to Mr. Watkins and said, "I trust this will cover it."

Mr. Watkins counted the money before he nodded saying, "Yes, absolutely. Thank you for stopping here. Can I tempt you with some of my famous coconut candy?" He said as followed them to the door.

William looked at Catherine again.

"No. No, thank you," she said.

William opened the door and held it as Catherine walked out.

Outside, she turned and faced him. "Thank you for an enjoyable lunch. I am looking forward to Sunday afternoon." Catherine held out her hand. William took her hand, leaned down and kissed it.

"Thank you for your company. It too made my lunch more enjoyable. And I am also looking forward to Sunday."

William put his hat on and said, "Until Sunday."

Catherine smiled before she turned and walked away. William stood watching her as he pulled out his pocket watch. He opened the watch and quickly turned towards the trolley stop. If he missed this trolley, he would be late for his meeting.

William whistled as he hustled towards the stop. He couldn't recall the last time he whistled.

CHAPTER 6

"What brings you out so early?" Chloe asked her brother, John, as she filled the teakettle with water. She carried it to the stove, lit the burner and placed it down. Chloe retrieved two cups and saucers from the shelf. As she reached for the metal tin filled with tea, John answered her.

"I have news. I am afraid it ain't good news. Not good at all. They have arrested Jacob," John said. "They have arrested Jacob for the murders of Grace and Timmy."

Bang! The metal tea cannister fell to the floor and its contents spilled out.

"What? Jacob killed them? No, I don't believe it."

John jumped from the chair to pick up the canister and help his sister to a chair. He grabbed the broom and swept up the tea leaves.

"They arrested him. I ran into Detective Maloney earlier and he told me. They were on their way to the farm to tell father." John continued, "I don't think he could do it. I'm going downtown to hire this attorney. I stopped in to see McNally; he gave me the name of a good lawyer. Hammil, Robert Hammil."

"Do you have the money for an attorney?" Chloe knew Catherine Landers made weekly payments to Tom's attorney. "Will they let us make payments?"

"I have enough for a retainer."

"I will talk to Charles to see if we can help too."

Whew-whew! The teapot whistled.

Chloe quickly rose and lifted the teapot. She poured the water into the cups and handed one to John.

"Honey or sugar?"

"Honey, please." Chloe took the honeypot off the shelf and carried it to the table. John lift the lid and drizzled honey into his tea. He stirred it before he took a sip.

The siblings talked over tea. Chloe asked John how his wife, Emma was feeling. Like Chloe, she was expecting, but it was their second. Baby Timmy was six months-old and kept Emma on her toes.

John inquired on Chloe's health. Chloe showed John the cradle Charles was making. John admired his handiwork.

When John had finished his tea, he rose to leave. He glanced at the cuckoo clock on the wall and said, "The next trolley leaves in fifteen minutes, I better hurry, or I will miss it."

He kissed his sister on the cheek and left.

Chloe fell back into the rocking chair. Jacob? No. He wouldn't do that to mama. He couldn't.

Chloe rocked for a few minutes thinking about her brother. She knew their father wouldn't help him. Papa would offer a rope, she thought knowing how devastated her father was over Timmy's death. Though he didn't care two licks about Gracie. Chloe saddened as she thought about her sister. Their deaths left a void in her heart.

Suddenly, Chloe sat up straight. She carefully pushed herself up. She wanted to go to the police station. She felt the need to see Jacob. She thought he needed to know they would support him.

She grabbed her shawl from a hall tree. She wrapped it around her shoulders and tied it at her neck. She grabbed her hat and left the house.

* * * * * * * * *

Anna Belle removed the clothes from the line. With each item, she detached the pins and dropped them into a bag handing on the line. She held up each item shaking it to remove any creases. Then she folded it, placed in the wicker basket at her feet and moved to the next item. She sighed at the full basket. It meant an afternoon of standing over a hot iron starching her husband's shirts.

As she removed the last shirt, she felt a rumbling deep in her belly. Not a labor pain but a hunger pang.

Grr, grr! Her stomach growled.

She looked up to the sky and smiled to herself. Her baby knew it was noon. She picked up the basket and carried it to the house. Balancing the basket on one hip, she used her other hand to open the door. Once inside, she placed the basket on the floor next to the washing machine and made herself–and her baby–supper.

The house already warm from the spring sun. Anna Belle opened the icebox; the chilly air offered relief from the heat. She contemplated heating soup but decided on a cold meat sandwich instead.

Anna Belle made a sandwich and washed it down with lemonade. When she had finished, she cleaned up her dishes. She wiped the sweat from her brow. I had better open the windows before it gets too hot in here.

Rap-rap-rap!

"Who could that be?" she said. She wondered if she had forgotten an engagement.

Opening the door, her older sister, Chloe, surprised her.

"Did we have plans this afternoon?" she asked stepping aside, so her sister could come in.

"No. I must tell you something. It is not good news."

"Please sit down. Can I get you something to drink?"

"No, thank you. Something terrible happened."

Oh, no. Our family can't take more sad news. "Mama? Papa? What? Please tell me."

"John stopped by this morning. They have arrested Jacob." Chloe continued, "for Grace and Timmy's murder."

Anna Belle placed her hand to her mouth then said, "What? When?"

"Today." The both knew what day it was–the first anniversary of the murders of their brother and sister.

"John went in downtown to hire a lawyer. Mr. McNally gave him the name of an attorney. I want to go see Jacob." Chloe continued, "Anna, I don't think Jacob would do it. We all know he and Papa fought but kill Timmy. And Gracie? I don't believe it. Do you?"

"No, I don't think he could either. When are you going?"

"Right now."

"I want to come with you too. Let us go!" Anna Belle said as she stood up. She grabbed her shawl from a hook by the door.

A few minutes later, Chloe and Anna Belle stood in front of the police station. Like their brother, they had never seen the inside.

Apprehensively, the pregnant sisters climbed the few steps to the door. At the top, Chloe pulled on the heavy door and stepped inside. The both recognized the officer at the large raised desk. Behind him, an empty squad room.

It wasn't a very spacious room. The room sparsely furnished. In the center, a large desk with papers scattered on top. A few wooden chairs randomly placed around the room. Another desk pushed up against the wall. Nothing but an inkwell on top. Uncovered windows allowed light to enter. After dark, the light that hung from the ceiling illuminated the room. The walls were bare, except for a picture of President Roosevelt and a clock with a pendulum swung back and forth.

Anna Belle leaned towards her sister and whispered, "I wonder where they have Jacob."

"Back there," Chloe said nodding towards a closed door in the back.

"Can I help you?" O'Reilly bellowed startling the women.

"Um, yes, um… I was wondering if, by any chance, I mean, I would like to speak to someone in charge. I understand you arrested my, our brother, um, Jacob n' uh, we would like to see him."

"If you take a seat, Detective Maloney should be back shortly."

"Where is he?" Anna Belle blurted out.

"Please, ladies! Take a seat. The detective should be back soon," O'Reilly pleaded. He watched as they took a seat in the chairs against the wall then looked back down at his newspaper. He could hear the sisters whispering but couldn't make out what they were saying.

An hour later, O'Reilly wondered where Maloney and Morrow were. They should have been back hours ago.

"Officer! Excuse me, officer!" Chloe called out. "Should they not have been back by now?"

"Yeah, I'm not sure why the delay. Maybe you should come back."

Chloe suddenly remembered she hadn't eaten since breakfast and it was mid-afternoon.

"I need to run to the shops, and we will come back shortly."

What?? Chloe wants to shop now! Anna Belle knew her sister liked to shop, but this wasn't the time or place to shop.

"Let's go!"

Anna Belle followed her sister outside. When they were outside, she placed her hand on her sister's shoulder and spun her around then asked, "You want to shop? Now?"

Chloe giggled, "Oh, no, silly. I'm hungry. Or my baby is. I haven't eaten since breakfast. I want to run to the bakery for a sweet roll."

Anna Belle laughed and hooked her arm in to her sister's. The two pregnant women a sight as they walked to the bakery.

Inside the bakery, the sweet scents of fresh-baked goods caressed their senses.

"Yummy! Now, I'm hungry too!" Anna Belle exclaimed.

The two sisters eyed the display cabinet. Fresh baked rolls, breads and cookies neatly arranged on trays tempted them.

The bakery owner greeted them, "Good afternoon! How can I help you?"

"I want one of each!" Chloe said with a smile. "But I think I will just have a slice… no, a cookie, no, I think I want… I don't know. It all looks so good."

"I think, I will have a slice of apple cider cake, please," Anna Belle said.

"That sounds delicious! I will have a slice too. Please."

The baker opened the back of the cabinet and used a spatula to remove two slices. He placed on the plates and set on the counter.

"Would you like anything to drink?" he asked. "I have freshly squeezed lemonade in the icebox. Or tea?"

Anna Belle thought about the lemonade for a second. "I think I'll have a cup of tea, please."

"I will too."

The baker rang up the sale and said, "Ten cents, please."

Chloe opened her satchel and retrieved a dime. She stopped Anna Belle from reaching into her own satchel.

"My treat," she said to her sister.

A small round table sat in the corner by the large display window. The sisters carried their cake to the table and took their seats. A minute later, the baker brought their tea.

"Thank you, ladies! Enjoy!"

After he stepped away, Anna Belle said, "Do you know what you will say to Jacob?"

"Gosh, I hadn't thought about that. I know I want to see him. To let him know we are standing behind him. God only knows, how Papa will react!"

"Yeah, let him know we will help him." Anna Belle continued, "I forgot to tell you. I felt something this morning. Not a labor pain. But a pain like Mama told us. It's too early."

"Why didn't you tell me this sooner? I wouldn't have let you leave the house! Robert will be madder than a wet hen when he finds out I had you parading all over town in your condition."

"First, I only had one or two and I was washing clothes. Lifting baskets of wet clothes to hang outside. And Robert doesn't know."

"Promise me if you have any more you will tell me!"

"Yes, I promise. Don't you be worrying about me. You have your own baby to worry about."

"You are my sister and I love you and I want the best for you."

"I said I promised. And you too!"

"I will. Mama says the Snyder women are good at breeding babies. It's too bad papa said nothing about his family."

"He's never mentioned them. Do you think he ever wrote letters?"

"Papa never learned to read or write. So, it is doubtful he ever did. And if he wanted to, he would have to find someone who could read and write Swedish. I only know a few words just from Papa talking or yelling."

Chloe giggled as she thought about her father's own language; a mixture of English and Swedish. But if something angered Papa, he only spoke Swedish.

"I miss the ol' papa. He hasn't been the same since Timmy's and Gracie's death. Papa had a jolly laugh. I miss hearing it."

"You mean, just Timmy. He never cried over Gracie."

"Yeah, since someone killed Timmy. He doesn't smile anymore."

"Poor John and Emma. It's like Baby Timmy doesn't exist. And they named him after Timmy."

"Yeah, Papa just calls him *the baby*." Anna Belle sighed. "Speaking of names, have you and Charles thought about names?"

"If it's a boy, Charles, of course. But we haven't agreed on a girl's name. He likes the traditional names, Mary or Sarah and I want something not so common, Sophia or Susannah."

"I like all of those names. We're still deciding too. For a girl's name. Robert if it's a boy."

"Ya better choose one soon. You have little time left before that baby will be here."

The girls continued talking about baby things, eating their cider cake, and drinking their tea.

When they had finished, Chloe said, "Surely, the detective should be back by now. We better hurry back."

The girls hooked arms and made their way back to the police station.

CHAPTER 7

David hitched up the mule to the plow. His employer, Mr. Murphy wanted his acreage plowed and ready to plant by the end of April. Like Mr. Murphy, the old mule had seen better days. He'd be lucky if it made it through this year.

David steered the plow to the field. He had hours of plowing ahead of him and it was mid-morning. He might have to skip his noon meal to finish today. After breakfast, Mrs. Murphy made a meat pie for supper. *She sure makes great meat pie!* He thought. *If I hurry, I still might enjoy it.*

For next few hours, David followed the mule across the field; turned around and back again. Up and back. The monotonous work allowed him to think about his dreams. His future.

His future looked a little brighter after last week. Unexpectedly, Mr. Murphy asked him to stay seated after their supper. Mrs. Murphy cleared away their dirty dishes and poured more coffee in their mugs.

"David," he said. "I ain't getting' any younger. N' I ain't got any male heirs. My two daughters married well 'n don't need this land. We got that farmhouse in the back forty. We kin fix it up for a family."

"Just ask him already," Mrs. Murphy said.

"I'm gettin' there, ole woman."

"David, would you want to be our tenant farmer?" she blurted out.

"Betsy, I said I was getting there," Mr. Murphy said. "Would you want that, boy? We'll change our will so that you'd git all the land when we are gone. And this house too. But not all the furnishings."

"Sum' of them r' 'airlooms n' our daughters want them," Mrs. Murphy added.

David's jaw dropped. It was something he dreamed about since he was a small boy. His parents once owned a farm just north of town. A family farm can withstand one dry summer but couple it with flooding the next year and it was a disaster. Eventually, his father was forced to borrow money from the local savings and loan to survive but heavy rains and flash floods washed away their crops. With no money to pay back the note, the bank foreclosed, and forced David's family to move out.

Even though he was just a little boy, he remembered that day well. The knock on the door. The look on his papa's face as he talked to the men in dark suits. The way his mama cried as she closed the door for the last time. They packed up what little possessions they had left and moved to Des Moines. Unable to find work and with no money to rent a home, the family moved to the poor farm.

With his farming experience, David's father strived there. In just three years, he had saved almost enough money for them to move out. Plans were in place for them to move out the following spring, but tragedy struck again. That winter, both his parents contracted influenza and died at the Poor Farm. David was just ten years old.

None of the other residents of the poor farm wanted another mouth to feed, so they contacted the Des Moines Home for Friendless Children. David waited for someone from the orphanage to pick him up, but heavy snow storms delayed their trip for weeks.

Hearing of the orphan boy, Betsy and Jeb Murphy traveled to the Poor Farm and offered to give him a home. With just two daughters, the Murphy family jumped at the chance to have a son. For David, anything was better than an orphanage. They provided him with a place to sleep, fed and clothed him and sent him to school. After school, Jeb taught David about farming. Two years later, David completed the eighth-grade; Jeb's arthritis made it difficult for him to handle the daily chores, so David took over the farm chores under Mr. Murphy's watchful eye. Mr. Murphy still ran things. His legs might not work but he had no trouble barking out orders.

The twelve-year-old boy rose at dawn and worked until the sun set. Mrs. Murphy treated him like a son, but they never legally adopted him. A few years later, David moved out of the main home and set up a room in the barn. This gave him the privacy he yearned for.

"So whatcha say, boy?"

"Gosh, yes!"

David looked out over the acreage. Someday this will be mine. All mine!

"David! Dave!" he heard from afar.

Looking up, he saw his friend, Harry standing by the gravel road; he waved his hat high above his head.

David pushed the mule to meet his friend.

"Harry!" he yelled out to his friend when he was close to him. He stopped the mule and walked over to him. "What are you doing here?"

"Bad news. They arrested Jacob. Today. For the murders of his brother and sister."

"What? He didn't do it! We know that!"

"I heard his brother, John went downtown to hire an attorney for him. He will need bail money. I got some saved. You got any?"

"Yeah. I can help. I got to finish plowing before I can go anywhere. Old man Murph will be angry if I don't get it done."

"Word is they will take Jacob downtown in the morning for his a… a… arraignment. We got time."

"I should be done mid-afternoon. 3 or 4. I must let Mrs. Murphy know about supper." Even after all the years of living with the Murphy's, he still referred to them as Mr. and Mrs.

"I will meet you in front of the police station about half past four."

"See ya later, Harry!"

David started the plow again. He moved swiftly this time. He had an important deadline. Now, David's thoughts turned to his friend. He knew Jacob didn't do it.

"I remember that night well."

Engrossed in his thoughts, David didn't realize he had finished the field. *That ought a please Murph.*

Meanwhile, Detective Maloney opened the door to the stable. He peered in. Behind him, the neighbor and caretaker looked over his shoulder. With only a few rays of sunshine peering through missing boards, the barn was dark.

"Duke!" Maloney whispered loudly. He scanned the barn for the mutt.

Woof!

"Duke. Where are you, boy?"

Woof!

Maloney took a few more steps in to the stable.

"Look! Over there!"

Duke lay facing them. In front of Duke, Lucas laid on his stomach. He lay motionless. Duke's head rested on his master's back.

Maloney ran and knelt next to the man. He placed his hand on his shoulder and rolled him over. He gasped when he saw the shotgun hidden under him. He scanned the man's torso for a wound, blood, something.

"Lukas! Lukas! Answer me, Lukas!"

Outside, Claire heard Maloney cries.

"Lukas is in the stable?" she exclaimed as she rose to go to him.

"Wait!" Morrow reached out and grabbed her arm to hold her back. He didn't want Claire running into the barn until he knew what they found inside.

"Let me go!" She shook arm to release his hold. "Lukas! Are you in there? Answer me, Lukas!" She ran towards the barn. Tears filled her eyes.

* * * * * * * * *

Three and four-story buildings lined Court Avenue. John glanced the numbers over the doors as he walked. John looked up at the large numbers etched into the glass above the large oak doors.

"Three hundred Court. This is the place."

John grunted as he opened the heavy door. Once inside, he removed his hat, ran his fingers through his hair and tucked his shirt into his pants.

Inside, John looked at the building directory handing on the wall. He reviewed the names until he found "Robert Hammil, Second Floor, Room 5." Taking two steps at a time, John climbed the stairs to the second floor then walked down the hall. He looked at each door and stopped briefly to read the name on the window. At the end of the hall, he reached room five.

In black block letters, "Robert Hammil, Esquire" painted on the front. John opened the door and walked in.

Behind a desk, an older woman sat opening mail. "May I help you?" She slipped the knife-like device into the envelope flap and with a flick of her hand, it glided across the top and tore open the mail.

"I would like to, uh, hire, no talk, to Mr. Hammil, please. I need to hire him to defend my brother."

"Let me see if he is available. Please take a seat."

She stood up, smoothed out her gray skirt and walked to the door. She knocked lightly and in a soft voice said, "Mr. Hammil?" John heard a faint "come in" as he took a seat and looked around the sparsely decorated room. He sat down in one of the leather-upholstered chairs. He rested his hands on the leather-padded arms, he ran his fingers over the brass grommets holding the materials together. Across the room, the snow-covered peaks of a mountain range seemed old to John. He had never seen mountains in person; just read about them in school.

Eleven fifteen. Jacob has been in jail for a few hours already. John thought as he looked at the large clock on the wall behind him.

Click. A closing door interrupted his thoughts. John looked up to see the secretary return to the room.

"If you can wait, Mr. Hammil will see you in a few minutes." She took her seat at the desk.

"Yes. I will."

John picked up the daily newspaper sitting on the table next to him. He scanned the headlines; a wagon overturn in Valley Junction, a local church holding their spring bazaar the following Sunday, and a

Highland Park business owner announced his intention to run for office.

I wonder how much longer; he thought as he glanced back at the clock.

As if she read his mind, the secretary "Mr. Hammil will see you soon," she said.

"Thank you."

Suddenly, the door opened. A short robust man stood in the doorway. His salt and pepper hair slick back. Long sideburns edged his cheek line stopping at his chin. He wore dark black pants with a silver and white striped vest over a white-collared shirt. The sleeves rolled up exposing his pale skin. No farmer's tan on him.

"Please come in," he said to John.

John stood up and walked towards the door. He held out his right hand and said, "John Johansson."

Robert Hammil reached out his hand and shook John's. John noticed the attorney's soft hands; another dead giveaway he wasn't a farmer.

"Johansson! Robert Hammil," he replied as he stepped aside for John to enter.

John walked into the room. This room contrasted with the waiting room. Dark walnut shelves jam packed with green and brown leather-bound books. A large desk in the middle flanked by two windows that expanded to the ceiling. A layer of winter muck covered the panes obstructing the view.

The attorney spoke first.

"Johansson, you say? Are you related to the Johansson children that were murdered last year?" The Tom Landers' trial fresh on his mind. Like many attorneys, he watched the trial from the galley and took notes on the triumphs or failures of both sides of the courtroom. As an acquaintance of both attorneys, Robert tried to keep neutral; but as a defense attorney, he rooted for William McNally.

"Yes, they were my younger brother and sister."

"How can I help you today? You say you need to hire an attorney?"

"Yes. For my brother. William McNally referred me."

"McNally. Good man. Good attorney. He was the one who defended the Landers kid."

"Yes." Not wanting to waste any more time, he continued, "My brother, they arrested him, Jacob Johansson for the murders of my siblings. I want to hire you to represent him."

The attorney's forehead wrinkled as he thought for a minute. He mentally reviewed the cases he was working on. A few criminals but they were minor charges. This trial could make or break me, he thought as he recalled how McNally's popularity skyrocketed after his successful defense.

"I will take your case," he said. He grabbed the ink pen out of the holder and dipped into the inkwell. "I need a few details."

The attorney asked John a few questions; John offered as much information as he knew. By the time they finished, it was half-past twelve.

"I need to get back to see my brother. What happens now?"

"The police will eventually transport your brother downtown to the main jail. Later today or early in the morning. It is across the street from the courthouse. There will be an arraignment. They will formally charge him. I will find out when and meet him at the courthouse. After his arraignment, I will work on his defense. One more question, bail? Do you have money for bail?"

"I have some. And my sisters will help too. How much will it be?"

"It's hard to say. Tom Landers' bail was five hundred dollars; I'm expecting about the same."

John nodded.

"And I will need a retainer. You or he can make payments until the trial."

"Jacob has a farm and is employed by the creamery in Highland Park. He won't make any money if he sits in jail."

"No, he won't. I will do my best to have him released on bail."

John rose and reached across the desk. He shook the attorney's pudgy hand and said, "My brother didn't do it."

I heard that before, the attorney thought before saying aloud, "I will do everything in my power to defend him."

Satisfied he had made the right decision hiring Attorney Hamill, John bid goodbye and left the office. He raced down the staircase and stepped outside.

The afternoon sun warmed the spring air. John rushed down the street towards the train stop. If he hurried, he could still catch the one-o'clock trolley to Highland Park. He still hadn't seen his brother and it would be mid-afternoon before he made it to the police station. The news of an attorney might ease Jacob's worries.

A few miles north, Jacob paced in his cell. Four steps to front, then he turned and took four steps to back wall. Repeatedly. Over and over.

For the past few hours, Jacob tried to remember what happen that night. He remembered being angry at his father. He remembered taking one too many swigs of the whiskey.

He remembered waking up in his house but not knowing how he got there. He remembered a new tear in his shirt; unsure where or how he did it. And that pounding headache and hearing the news of his brother and sister's death. He remembered stopping several times that morning on his creamery route to vomit.

What did I do that night? he asked himself. I don't remember what happened. He wished he could send a message to his friends; the ones that were at the river that night, to asked them what happened.

On the bench, a tray held the remains of his supper. A few remnants of a sandwich lay next to the half-eaten apple. Jacob's usual robust appetite replaced with a stomach tied in knots; just the thought of food nauseated him. He kept down part of his dinner but worrying took the best of him.

Jacob continued pacing. His pacing wore out a path on the beaten down dirt floor. He continued to try to remember the events that night. Too many swigs of hooch! Since moving to his farm and courting Isabelle, he hadn't had an ounce of liquor.

I must talk to David and Harry.

Why hasn't anyone come to see me? Surely by now, Mama or John or the girls knows I'm here.

What time is it? Jacob tried to guess how long he had been in the cell since there were no windows in the basement. Four or five hours. It must be at least one.

Jacob heard the ringing of the telephone. He heard someone talking but with the floor between them, he couldn't make out what they said. Just muffled voices. He knew it was the desk officer since the other two hadn't returned yet.

Jacob sat down on the bench hoping someone would come to talk to him. He heard more footsteps. They seemed to cross the room.

* * * * * * * * *

John jumped off the trolley. He walked swiftly hoping to see Jacob and give him the news about Hammil. Afterwards, he needed to head back home. He had used a telephone at the feed and seed store to let Emma know the reason for his delay. She would have worried. And in her condition, she didn't need that. He hoped she didn't have her hands full with a fussy baby and Timmy napped for a few hours to allow her to rest.

"John, John!" he heard from behind him. He turned to see his two sisters walking arm in arm towards him.

He laughed at the sight of the pregnant women waddling

towards him. He knew better to tease them about the large bellies. His own wife's pregnancy made him more aware of the difficulties of childbirth. With three babies due over the next few months, their children would grow up together. He wished he would have had cousins, but six siblings provided him with all the entertainment he needed.

"What are you girls doing out?" he asked.

"We were going to see Jacob, but the Detective wasn't around. They told us to come back in an hour."

"We just had some delicious apple cider cake from the Highland Park Bakery. Yum!" Anna Belle said.

John realized he hadn't eaten since breakfast.

"I hired an attorney. He will meet Jacob at his arraignment. I'm on my way to see Jacob myself. He has to be worried."

"They have to let us see him now."

Miles away at the Johansson farm, Claire bit her fingernail as she waited for Detective Maloney or someone, anyone to come out of the barn with news.

Was Lukas hurt?

Finally, she saw their neighbor at the barn door. He motioned for the chief to join them. Claire followed.

"Please, Claire, stay here. I want to see first."

Claire reluctantly sat back down on the bale of hay, she closed her eyes and clasped her hands together. Please, Almighty God, keep my Lukas safe and alive. I ask of you. Amen.

Claire opened her eyes but quickly shut them. And Jacob too. Keep my son safe.

Opening her eyes again, she stared at the closed barn door.

Why are they not coming out? I need to know about Lukas. Claire finally stood up and ran to the barn. She stopped before opening it.

Claire leaned against the door and listened. She heard muffled voices calling her husband's name. She didn't hear her husband's voice.

Inside, Detective Maloney and Chief Morrow knelt next to Lukas' body. "Lukas, please talk to us."

They scanned his body. There were no obvious injuries; no blood; no mangled bones. He lay there staring into space.

Detective Maloney leaned down towards his face and said, "He's breathing! He's alive."

Outside, Claire heard the cries. She burst into the stable and called out to her husband. "Lukas! Lukas!"

Chief Morrow turned towards Claire, "Get Doc Baker. He's alive. But not responding."

Claire looked from the wagon to the horse. It would take her a while to hitch up the wagon. Finally, Joe said, "I'll go."

Detective Maloney said, "Who has a telephone around here?"

"The Davis' do," Claire replied.

Joe jumped into his wagon and with a snap of the reins, the horse took off. Claire watched as he disappeared over the horizon.

She stood leading against the barn door. She took in a deep breath and sighed. Please, God, heal my Lukas.

Chief Morrow opened the barn door startling Claire. "Is he going to live?" she asked hesitantly.

"We will have to wait until Doc Baker gets here. There are no obvious wounds. I'm not sure what is ailing him. Possibly apoplexy; a stroke."

"A stroke? Oh, no." Claire saddened as she remembered her uncle's struggle after suffering a stroke many years ago. Unfortunately, that led to his demise a short while later.

"Claire, we won't know anything until the doctor arrives. Let's not jump to conclusions," Morrow said. "We need to wait for the doctor."

From a distant, they heard the cries of the neighbor.

"What's he saying? I can't make it out."

"Doc Baker is on his way! He's on his way!"

"Thank God!" Claire exclaimed looking up towards the blue skies.

"Eliza Davis wanted to come with me. I told her to wait until we know more."

Eliza will worry. I will visit with her when I know more, Claire thought.

The pounding of hooves on the gravel road announced another wagon coming from the other direction. Chief Morrow and Claire turned towards the sounds.

"It's Doc Baker!" Claire ran to meet the wagon.

"Come quick, Doctor. Something is terribly wrong with Lukas. Help him, please!"

Dr. Baker slowed down his wagon near the barn and jumped down when it came to a complete stop.

"He's in the barn!" Morrow motioned the doctor to follow him.

Dr. Baker followed the police chief into the barn; he tried to close the door behind him, but Claire pushed it back open. It was her husband laying on the ground and she refused to be shut out.

Inside, Dr. Baker crouched down next to Lukas. "Lukas, Lukas. Please talk to me if you can."

He grabbed Lukas' hand. "Squeeze my hand if you can."

Dr. Baker waited a few seconds before repeating, "Squeeze my hand if you can hear me. Come on, Lukas, you can do this."

Dr. Baker finally noticed the shotgun lying by his side. "Is he shot?" he asked. Chief Morrow shook his head. "Not that we can see," he replied. The doctor scanned Lukas' body for injuries. No obvious ones.

"Are you hurt?"

Still nothing.

"Lukas, can you hear me?"

They all stood watching. Their hands clasped in front of them waiting and hoping for a sign from Lukas.

Finally, as they all watched, he moved his thumb; barely, but it moved.

"He moved! His thumb! It moved! Didn't it, Doc?" Claire exclaimed.

"We need to get him to the hospital right away."

"What's wrong with him?" Claire asked.

"I don't know. Could be a stroke. We need to get him to the hospital right away. No time to wait for the ambulance. At the hospital, I can examine him better," Dr. Baker replied looking around the barn. A woolen blanket hung over a stall partition.

"Over there, that blanket. Grab it! We can use that to carry him to my wagon."

Maloney jumped up and retrieved the blanket. He laid it down next to Lukas.

The doctor moved so he could lift Lukas' shoulders while the detective picked him up by his ankles. Once on the blanket, the four men carefully carried it out of the stable and placed him in the wagon's back.

The doctor jumped in the wagon's front, grabbed the reins, and took off. They stood there watching the wagon speed off.

Chief Morrow finally broke the silence saying, "I need to call

Officer O'Reilly; who did you say has a telephone?" The last part directed at the neighbor.

"The Davises do; about a half a mile down the road."

The police chief looked at Claire. "I need to get back to the station. I have police work to tend to, but I can meet you at the hospital after I call the station."

Claire knew what he meant by police work. He needed to charge her son with murder and transport him to the county jail downtown.

The policemen hopped into their wagon and headed westward on Madison towards the Davises leaving Claire standing there confused.

Should she had gone with the doctor? He didn't give a chance to react. She knew his concern was for Lukas.

Now, she really wished she knew how to hitch up the wagon.

I reckon I will walk to the hospital. Lillian is there. Her betrothed can bring me home later if he isn't on duty.

"Mrs. Johansson?" Joe interrupted her thoughts. "I can give you a ride to the hospital. I need to come back and take care of my cattle. But I can come back after supper to fetch ya."

"That would be so kind of you. Let me get my shawl and hat from inside the house." Claire walked fast, then lifting her skirt, sprinted to the house. Inside, she grabbed her shawl and hat from the hooks by the door. She placed her shawl over her shoulders and tied her bonnet under her chin. Grabbing her satchel, she ran out the door.

Meanwhile, the neighbor found a wooden box for to help Claire climb into the wagon. Once settled in the wagon's front, he moved the box and climbed in next to her. With a flick of his wrists, the wagon jolted forward.

They rode in silence leaving Claire to her thoughts and prayers.

Please God, keep my family safe. Please heal whatever ails Lukas. Protect Anna Belle and Chloe's babies. And Emma too. Help me understand why I said what I did about the murderer of my children.

Do I really think Jacob could kill them? Yes, he was mad that night but not at the children. He was mad at his father. He would have killed his father before he killed Gracie and Timmy. Jacob wouldn't have hurt me like that. Why didn't I keep my thoughts to myself?

* * * * * * * * *

Ring-ring-ring! The telephone on the detective's desk rang. Half asleep, O'Reilly jumped at ringing.

He sauntered over to the desk and answered the telephone. "Highland Park Police Station."

"O'Reilly, this is Chief. This will delay us longer. Emergency at Johansson's. Lukas is on his way to Mercy Hospital. Has anyone showed up to see our prisoner?"

"Yes, his brother and two sisters were here. I told them to come back. What should I tell 'em?"

"Let them see him. We will try to get back in about an hour. You better tell them about their father too."

"Will do, sir!"

"I'm not sure how much more this family can take."

"Yes, Sir."

O'Reilly placed the earpiece on its hook and walked back to his desk.

Meanwhile, Anna Belle, Chloe, and John stood in front of the police station ready to climb the steps.

"I'm demanding to see Jacob this time," John said.

"Yes, we must see him!" his sisters chimed in unison.

They climbed the few steps to the door. John opened the door and held it for his sisters. He followed them. Inside, they found Officer O'Reilly standing by the telephone. He placed the mouthpiece on his hook and walked to the front desk. He looked up at them.

Before he could greet them, John bellowed, "I, we demand to see Jacob."

O'Reilly stood. "Right this way. But." He stopped in his tracks. "The detectives are not back. There was an emergency at your parents' farm. Your father is on his way to Mercy Hospital."

"Oh, no!" Anna Belle exclaimed. Chloe gasped as she raised her hand to her mouth.

"What happened?"

"That's all I know. They don't know."

John followed his sisters behind the desk. O'Reilly retrieved the key to the cell, opened a door and motioned for them to follow him. They descended the stairs to the basement.

A lone gas lamp gave light to the dreary room. They saw their brother sitting on the bench, his head resting in his hands, his blonde hair tousled. He looked up when he heard the door close.

"Jacob!" the three siblings cried out.

"Oh, gosh, am I glad to see you three? I don't know what I will do."

"Shh!" John placed his index finger in front of his mouth as he eyed the officer standing there.

O'Reilly unlocked the cell allowing the three to enter. He locked it behind them and pointed to a bell between the cells. "Ring that when you are finished."

They waited until he had disappeared to say anything.

Jacob hugged them at the same time. Chloe thought, unusual behavior for Jacob.

"Sit down." Jacob pointed to the bench. Chloe and Anna Belle took seats on the bench.

John remained standing. "I hired an attorney for you. Hammil. Robert Hammil. He comes highly regarded by McNally. He will meet you at the arraignment. The three of us have money for bail, about five hundred dollars, do you have any?"

"Yes, I have a tin can at my house with about a hundred. It was supposed to be for seeds. But I got some in the bank," But I ain't going to need it if I don't get out. I could buy seed on credit. I doubt the seed dealer would do that after this.

"What have they told you?"

"Not much. Just that I am charged with Timmy and Gracie's murder. And they will transport me to the county jail for the arraignment. They dumped me down here and left. Haven't been back since."

"Let's hope that you get out tomorrow."

"And we will pray too," Anna Belle piped in.

"You know, I haven't gone to church in over a year. I don't think God would listen to my prayers."

"Speaking of praying, there was an emergency at the farm. Papa is at the hospital now."

Jacob shrugged his shoulders. His indifference obvious. There was no love lost between them.

"I will have to get a message to Emma and head over to the hospital when we leave here."

"I want to go too."

"No, you two need to get home. Both your husbands will be home soon and wondering where you are."

Chloe sighed and shook her head slightly back and forth. But she knew he was right. She didn't leave a note and Charles would frantically search for her.

Anna Belle also nodded in agreement. Her baby was due soon

and Robert would search everywhere for her.

Chloe said, "I can telephone Emma when I get home."

"Thank you. That will save me time. Let her know I will be home as soon as I can."

"Jacob, do you want us to be at the court tomorrow? I could come with Robert in the morning."

Jacob looked at his sister. "I would appreciate it, but I think it's best you two stayed home. I mean, being with child."

Jacob's eyes welted. Even after years of aloofness, his siblings still cared for him.

Chloe noticed Jacob's eyes. She stood up, walked over to him, and leaned her head on his upper arm. "Jacob, you are blood, our brother and we love you. And we will stand by you through thick and thin. Just remember that."

"And we don't believe for a minute you killed Timmy and Gracie," Anna Belle added.

Jacob nodded, unable to speak with the lump building up in his throat.

John sensed Jacob's uneasiness. "The plan is that the attorney will be there for your arraignment. When the judge sets your bail, he will telephone me. I will bring the money to the courthouse for bail. Once they release you, you will sit down with the attorney and tell him everything you can remember."

"That's problem. I remember nothing that night. I remember going to the river and someone brought some hooch. That's it. The next thing I remember is waking up in my farmhouse." Jacob paused for a few seconds. "Can you get a message to Harry and David? They might be able to fill in my lost time."

"David lives at Murph's, right?"

"Yes, he does, but he sleeps in the barn. I mean, he has a room in the barn."

"I will stop there on my way home." John quickly corrected himself, "Oh, wait. Papa. I will stop to see David after I go to the hospital."

John stood up and slap his brother on the back. "Try to get sleep tonight. We will have you out of here tomorrow. "

"Jacob, Charles and I have an extra room. You can stay with us until this is over," Chloe said.

"I'll stay at my house."

"So close to Papa?" Anna Belle asked.

"Blast! I forgot about that. He will be crazy as a loon. What about my farm? How can I avoid him?"

"We will hash that out tomorrow. We need to get you out of here first. Chloe and Anna Belle need to go home. I want to find out what's wrong with Papa." John instructed them.

"And I need to check on Emma too!" Chloe piped in.

"Yes, I telephoned her this morning. I'm sure she is fretting about; concerned for everyone's safety." He added to Jacob, "try to sleep tonight. I will see you tomorrow morning."

Chloe and Anna Belle stood up. Chloe walked over to Jacob first. With just ten months' difference in age, she felt the closest to him. Their parents raised them together; like twins. They shared a special bond for years but drifted apart as they grew older. Jacob wrapped his arms around his sister and hugged her tightly. He loosened his arms when he remembered her condition.

"Oh, sorry about that."

"I'm good."

Since Anna Belle's belly protruded more, Jacob leaned down and gave her a quick hug around her shoulders.

"Thank you for coming."

John rang the bell hanging between the cells. They heard the footsteps of Officer O'Reilly as he walked towards the stairs. When he appeared on the landing, John whispered, "Try not to worry too much. We will help you fight this."

John followed his sisters out of the cell. Jacob stood in the middle of his cell and watched until they disappeared. His sisters never approved of his drinking, but their visit eased his worries. He was glad for his family's support or at least, half his family.

Upstairs, John asked Officer O'Reilly, "When will he be transported downtown?"

"It should have been this afternoon. At this late hour, not until the morning."

Outside, John hugged his sisters and promised to let them know their father's condition. Across the street, he recognized Jacob's friend, David.

CHAPTER 8

David quickly made his way to the barn. He unhitched the mule and led him into the stall leaving the plow outside.

David lifted the pump lever to wash his hands. He was glad they finally replaced the lever. The rusty old pump's shiny lever looked out of place.

Inside, Mrs. Murphy removed the corn bread from the oven and placed the hot pan on a trivet on her sideboard. Using her finger, she pressed a dimple into the top and watched it disappeared.

"David, I missed you at lunch. You must be starving."

"I was finishing the back forty. I didn't want to stop for lunch," he said.

"Want me to heat a bowl of soup for you?"

"Nah, I wanted to let you know I won't be here for supper either. I need to meet Harry at four thirty in Highland Park." He noticed the puzzled look on her face and added, "my friend, Jacob, was arrested. I want to visit him before they take him downtown. I will just grab a few of those biscuits from breakfast if that's fine with you."

"Yes, please. Take what you want. Should I split them and add mutton too?"

"No, thanks, just the biscuits should be enough."

Mrs. Murphy reached for basket on the shelf over the oven. She opened the cloth revealing two biscuits.

"There is just two left. Are you sure that be enough?" she said as she held the basket out for him.

"Yes, Mrs. Murphy. Thank you." David took the last two biscuits and left the house. David ate the biscuits as he headed towards Highland Park

Thirty minutes later, he stood outside the police station. He looked around for Harry. He didn't think Harry would go in alone.

David sat down on a bench across the street and waited. He thought about what he would say to Jacob.

The door to the police station opened and out walked two pregnant women and a taller man. David recognized Jacob's sisters and older brother.

He watched as John hugged his sisters. John look in his direction and recognized him as one of Jacob's friend.

"John!" he called out.

John looked back over and waved to David. He hugged his sisters again before walking towards David. As he reached David, he looked back at his sisters' leave, arm in arm. Since his wife had difficult pregnancies, he worried about his sisters' health too.

"Are you here to see Jacob? Jacob had asked me to get a message to you. He will be happy you are here."

David stood up and held his hand out. The men shook hands.

"Yes, I am waiting for Harry. We wanted to help with his bail. How's he doing?"

"Not good. It worries him. Nervous. It'll be good for him to see you. We won't know anything until tomorrow."

"What time is the arraignment?"

"First thing in the morning they will take him downtown. In the morning. I hired an attorney. The attorney I hired will call me after the judge sets bail to let me know how much it is. 'tween me an' my sisters, we have five hundred but if it is higher than that, I might call on ya! Still at Murph's?"

"Yeah," David answered. He continued, "I should be in the field tomorrow. Here's comes Harry now." He added seeing his friend walk towards them.

Harry walked up the men. The three talked for a few minutes before John left them.

When he was out of range, Harry pulled out his handkerchief and wiped his brow, "What did you tell him?"

"Nuttin.' I didn't say nuttin'."

"We better go in before it's too late."

They crossed the street and entered the building.

Inside, Officer O'Reilly sat reading the newspaper. He looked up and said, "Can I help ya?"

"We are here to see Jacob. Jacob Johansson."

"Follow me," O'Reilly stood up and walked to retrieve the keys.

In the basement, they saw their friend as he paced the tiny cell. O'Reilly didn't unlock the cell this time. He turned around before ascending the steps. "Ring the bell when you are finished, and I will unlock the door upstairs."

Jacob walked where his friends were standing. He held the bars in his hands and said, "Am I glad to see you? I remember nothing that night. Do you? Can you remember what happened?"

"Yeah, you were drunk as a skunk," David laughed.

"We had to help you home," Harry added.

"You did? I remember waking up wondering why I went to my house."

David and Harry took turns giving Jacob a rundown of the events from that night. "And we left you at your house," David finished.

"We went to the tavern in Highland Park." Harry added, "And I lost a good handkerchief that night too."

David shot Harry a dirty look.

"What happens tomorrow?" Harry asked.

"My arraignment. Downtown. That's where the figure out my bail. John hired me an attorney. Some bigwig."

"How much for the bail?" Harry asked.

"Tom Landers' bail was five hundred."

"Whew," Harry whistled. "Five hundred. They must think you're loaded."

"I have money saved. Saved for the seeds I ordered." Jacob sat down on the bench and placed his face into his hands.

* * * * * * * * *

"Mrs. Johansson, we are here."

Engrossed in her thoughts, Claire barely remembered any of the trip to hospital. It surprised her to see they had arrived already.

"Thank you. You have been kind."

"Just concerned for everyone's safety, Ma'am."

He jumped down and ran to other side to help Claire out of the wagon.

"I will be back to gitcha' after supper."

"I don't want to trouble you or your family. And Gertrude is home with all the children. She'll be worried sick."

"No problem, ma'am. Just neighbor helping neighbor. Last winter, you brought that soup when Gertrude was sick, ya nursed her 'til she was well. 'Member that? Neighbors helpin' neighbors. Nah, this ain't goin' to bother Gertrude one bit."

Claire smiled and turned to get down.

"Wait right there, ma'am!" He jumped down from the wagon and ran over to help Claire.

He held his hand out. Claire took his hand as she climbed down the side.

"You best get in there and find out what ails Lukas," he said.

He took his place in the wagon's front, snapped the reins and with a tip of his hat, he yelled back, "I see ya after supper."

Claire watched him ride away. I need to add his family to my prayers tonight. His mama raised him right.

Claire climbed the stairs into the hospital. She looked up to see a tired-looking nurse waiting at the top. A white apron covered her blue and white pinstripe shirt and dark blue skirt. Her beautiful blonde hair styled in a pompadour bun on top of her head with a white cap with a red stripe. It took Claire a minute to realize the nurse was her own daughter.

"Lillian, Papa…"

"I know, mama. I will take you to the parlor where you can wait. Benjamin, I mean, Dr. Carpenter," she looked around to see if anyone heard her. She continued, "Dr. Carpenter is with Doc Baker now. Follow me."

Claire followed her daughter, Lillian down the long hallway to a room at the end.

The tall windows along one wall allowed the sun to shine through and brightened the room. A tapestry couch sat across from the windows. Two solid chairs across from the couch allowed for many visitors.

"Mama, rest here while they examine Papa. Dr. Baker will come to see you when he finishes. I have a class now but will come back as soon as it is over."

* * * * * * * * *

In the examining room down the hall, Lucas lay on his back motionless on the table. He didn't moan in pain or utter any words, just stared up at the ceiling.

Dr. Baker stood over him. His stethoscope hung from around his neck. He reached up with both hands and grabbed the tubing, then moved it until tips were secure in his ears.

He placed the bell like end on Lukas' chest. He listened for a second or two. It sounded normal. Ba-bump! Ba-bump! He moved to the other side to listen to his lungs. "Lukas, can you take a deep breath for me"

"Hmm."

"What, Dr. Baker?" Dr. Carpenter asked.

"Nothing. His heart sounds normal. His breathing is normal. Take a listen for yourself."

Dr. Carpenter listened to his heart and lungs; he nodded in agreement. Everything appeared normal.

Dr. Baker took out a small hammer like object. He tapped on Lukas knee and it jerked.

"Hmm. His reflexes are normal too."

"I cannot detect any abnormality. I don't believe he is suffering from dropsy," Ben said when they both finished their examination.

"Everything appears normal. I think he needs to stay here at the hospital. Until he regains his motor skill."

"Put him in Lillian's ward. She will work the men's ward tonight."

"Good idea! While you move him, I will speak with Mrs. Johansson."

Dr. Baker left the examining room and headed towards the waiting room. There he found Claire standing by the window staring out at the street. Her arms folded in front of her. She turned when she heard the footsteps.

"Do you ever wonder about all the people walking by? Do you wonder if they are well? Their families in good health? Then I think about my life. How much has changed? We were a happy family. Our children healthy and ready to start their own lives. And then one day, it all changed. I lost two children, my husband is sick now and my son is in jail. I pray to God each day and night to bring my happy family back. I know it is God's will, but it's so hard, Dr. It's so hard."

Tears rolled down her cheeks. She opened her satchel for a hankie. Dr. Baker rushed over and pulled his handkerchief from his vest pocket. He handed it to Claire.

"I'm so sorry," she whispered as she dabbed her eyes with his handkerchief.

"It's all right, Claire." Dr. Baker understood her pain.

"How is Lukas?"

"He's still not responding. His heart is fine. No problems with his breathing. He has no injuries. No broken bones. He doesn't have the usual signs of dropsy. We are keeping overnight. Benjamin is moving him to a ward right now."

"Oh, he's staying?"

"Until he can walk or talk. We don't know what is wrong with him. We are putting him in Lillian's ward."

"Good, good. Lillian will watch over her papa tonight."

"She will have other patients, but most will sleep during the night. She might have time to sit with him after she completed all her duties for the night. Talk to him. I pray he will be better in the morning."

"Oh. Can I see him?"

"Yes, follow me."

Claire followed the doctor down the hall to a large staircase. Dr. Baker climbed the stairs two at a time and reached the top landing before Claire. He usually ran around at the hospital when visiting patients and had forgotten about Claire.

When Claire climbed the last step, he turned and directed her down the hall. As Claire walked, she peeked in the open doors. Inside, she could see several beds with patients sleeping or visiting with family members. Curtains hung across bars suspended from the ceiling; drawn to provide the patient with privacy as they bathed or changed to go home. A wooden chair and a table placed near the doorway; stacks of papers covered the top.

Each ward had a fireplace or stove to heat the room on chilly days and nights. The nurse's responsibilities included maintaining the heat. On cold nights, it meant several trips up and down the stairs with either their arms full of kindling or carrying buckets of coal. Floors swept; bed linens changed. A patient might need cold compresses or sponge baths until their fever broke.

Ward nurses were usually first- and second-year students. First-year students usually pulled the overnight shifts too; which explains why Lillian looked so tired. Classes held during the day; shift work overnight. Sleep came in small doses. A quick nap before classes and another one before she had to report for ward duty.

Dr. Baker stopped about halfway down the hall.

"In here." He held his arm out towards the open door.

Claire stepped inside. She scanned the beds and looked for her husband. Finally, she saw Ben help Lukas into the bed. He stepped aside when the doctor and Claire walked over.

"I think they settled him in. I need to check on a few other patients." Ben said as he turned to leave the ward.

Lukas laid on his back staring at the ceiling. The same blank look in his face. A blanket pulled up to his shoulders.

"Shall I?"

Dr. Baker nodded.

Claire walked to the side of the bed. A chair sat next to Lukas' bed. She sat down and reached for his hand.

"Lukas. Lukas, it's Claire," she whispered. "I don't know what is wrong, but I pray you get better. We've had a good life and so many more years to live."

Claire sighed when there was no response.

"We have grandbabies that are coming soon. Three more! John's baby boy is growing so fast. Remember how happy you were when our children were born."

Still nothing.

Claire looked up at Dr. Baker. He nodded for her to continue. He watched for any reaction from Lukas. Still nothing.

"Claire, continue to talk to him. I must check other patients as well." With that last statement, he turned to leave the ward.

For the next hour, Claire continued talking to Lukas. She talked about their children, including Grace and Timmy. She continued to talk about their growing family; one grandson and three more grandchildren in the next few months. She wasn't sure how long she had been talking. As her stomach growled, she thought, it must be close to suppertime. She glanced out the window. The sun had settled and the skies darkening.

Claire talked until her voice hoarse. She stared at her husband hoping to see him move. Her efforts were fruitless. He never acknowledged her. Exhausted, she had run out of things to say.

"Mama?" She felt a hand on her shoulder. She turned to see her eldest.

"John! I am glad to see you."

"What is wrong with Papa?"

"They don't know. He has to stay the night."

John pulled over a chair from the neighboring bed and sat down.

"John, I have tried talking to him. I pleaded with him. But he won't respond."

"Let me try," John said. He stood and walked around the bed. He crouched down at the head of the bed.

"Papa," he began, "it's John. Please let us help you. Please talk to us." He paused. They patiently waited for Lukas to respond but he didn't. He turned towards his mother. She motioned for him to continue.

John turned back to look at his father.

"Papa, you should see our baby boy. He's growing fast. Every day, it's a new trick. Crawling. Pulling himself. Playing pat-a-cake. And our new baby is due soon."

John purposely left out his son's name. He and Emma named their boy after John's brother but now regretted it. His papa refused to call the child, Timmy. To him, there would be only one Timmy. It hurt Emma so much she even talked about changing his name, giving their son a nickname or calling him the formal "Timothy."

Still nothing. He returned to his seat next to his mother and reached over to take her hand. They sat in silence and watched

Lukas.

John broke the silence. "Mama, I have to get back to Emma. I have been gone all day." Claire understood and nodded in agreement.

He stood up and Claire did too.

"Let's go over there a minute." John said as he motioned for his mother to join him. They stepped a few feet away from his bed.

"They had arrested Jacob today," John said.

"Yes, I know."

"You know? Does Papa?"

"I don't think he knows. Chief Morrow and Detective Maloney stopped over late this morning to tell him. I thought Papa was still in town but our neighbor, Joe saw him heading back to farm. But he didn't go to the farm. He went to the cemetery. The caretaker stopped by too. Lukas was acting crazy, yelling about seeing Timmy soon and it worried him."

"Mama. Could papa be crazy?"

"Oh, John. Don't say that! No, no, he isn't."

"They found his shotgun with him. Mama, do you think…"

"No, he wouldn't kill himself. Don't you say that! I heard him grumbling' about a fox around the chicken coop. He was trying to kill a stray fox or raccoon. I am sure."

"I'm sorry, Mama. I won't say anything again. I went to see Jacob today. Chloe and Anna Belle too."

"How is he?"

"I cannot lie. He's scared. The arraignment is in the morning. The three of us have enough for bail. Jacob has money saved too."

"Oh. How will he pay for the defense?"

"The attorney I hired, Robert Hammil, will take payments. Jacob needs to be out, so he can earn a living."

"Yes, he does. We won't be able to help. Lukas won't allow it."

"I know that."

"Oh, my," Claire laughed a bit. "If your father isn't crazy now, wait until after he finds out about Jacob."

"Until the trial is over, we have to keep the two apart. Jacob won't be helping with the milking. Can Daniel take on more chores?"

"He already has. We will speak to him."

"I need to get home. Emma is home, probably worrying right now."

"Yes, you need to go."

"I can take you home first."

"Oh, no. Our neighbor is coming back after his supper. I want to sit with your father longer."

"If you are sure, Mama, I will leave. I will be back in town tomorrow after the arraignment," John said as he stood. He leaned down to kiss his mother's cheek.

Claire stayed seated, her hands folder on her lap and watched over her husband. She didn't talk to him this time. His eyes were closed now. She could hear him breathing. He had fallen asleep.

Exhausted, both mentally and physically, Claire closed her own eyes. She recalled happier times. Lost in her thoughts, a familiar voice startled her.

"Mama."

"Lillian. What time is it?"

"Five o'clock. My shift is starting. I am serving supper soon. Do you think Papa will eat?"

"I don't know if he knows I am here. I think he is sleeping now."

"Dr. Baker gave him something to sleep. I don't think he will wake up for a while."

Lillian walked away; Claire watched her daughter at work. Carrying one at a time, she placed the trays on the tables next to the beds. She helped patients sit up then moved the tray to their laps.

Claire stood up and fussed with the blanket. She pulled it up to his chin and tucked the side under the mattress.

"Mama," Lillian interjected. "I'm supposed to do that. Why don't you let him rest? He might wake up in the wee hours of the morning, I will try to talk to him then. Most of the patients will sleep through the night."

Claire reluctantly stood and pushed the chair so that the seat was under the bed. "I'm sure that our neighbor is waiting for me outside. He was kind enough to return for me."

"I saw Joe White sitting in his wagon by the front steps. Don't worry, Mama, I will watch over him. If there is any change, I will send Benjamin with a word."

"I better not keep him waiting."

Claire reached out and hugged her daughter. Then quickly released her and thought it might have been inappropriate behavior. She didn't want Lillian reprimanded by the head nurse.

"Thank you."

"Of course, Mama! Now, hurry to catch your ride."

Claire walked across the room towards the door. Before exiting, she turned back and looked at Lukas. Please heal my dear husband.

Outside, she found Joe waiting in his wagon. "I hope I didn't rush you," he said as he jumped down to help her up.

Once seated, he reached back for a blanket. He handed it to Claire and said, "Here. Wrap this around you. The night air is chilly. "

"Thank you."

"Ma'am, I took the liberty and brought the cows in from the pasture and milked them. I heard about Jacob and all; I put the cans in the springhouse for ya, too."

"How will I ever repay you?"

"Ma'am, it's just neighbor helping neighbor."

Claire thought, how wonderful to have such a kind neighbor.

Thirty minutes later, he stopped the wagon in front of their farm and jumped out to help her.

"Please, take one or two of the milk cans home with you. You have a large family, many mouths to feed, and we have more than enough." With just a half a dozen cows, there wasn't enough to sell to the creamery and far too much for just Lukas and herself.

"That would be much appreciated. Do you need me to start a fire for ya?"

"I can manage. Thank you for your kindness. And send my love to Gertrude and the children."

"I will. And thank you for the milk."

Claire watched Joe walked towards the spring house. She opened the front door and entered the house. Claire turned on the switch and the room lit up. Thankful for the modern convenience. Claire removed her shawl and shivered. The house was cold from the cooler night air. In her haste to leave, she had forgotten to close the windows. Claire quickly closed the parlor window and walked into the kitchen. Her dirty teacup left on the table.

As she closed the kitchen window, she saw her neighbor carrying the metal can with fresh milk. He placed the can in the back of his wagon and climbed up on the bench. She made a note to share more milk with them.

Claire walked into the bedroom she shared with Lukas for over twenty-five years. She stood up and unbuttoned her blouse. She quickly removed her skirt and blouse and slipped the nightgown over her head. The white nightgown with a high neckline and long pleated sleeves skimmed the floor as she walked. Sitting down at the dressing table, she reached back and unpinned her hair. She shook her head and her golden locks fell to her shoulders. Picking up the silver-handled brush, she began her nightly ritual of one hundred strokes.

Claire mindlessly ran the brush through her hair as she stared at her reflection in the old mirror. A few gray hairs appeared around her crown over the past year. Her eyes no longer bright; instead, they looked tired with dark circles underneath. The past year had taken its toll on her. Claire placed the brush down and pick up her Bible. She quickly turned the pages until she found the right verse.

Claire whispered as she read, "Be strong and courageous. Do not be afraid or terrified because of them, for the Lord your God goes with you; he will never leave you nor forsake you."

She closed her Bible and held it to her chest. She closed her eyes; her lips moved as she repeated the prayer.

Claire placed the Bible down on the table. She placed her nightcap on her head.

Turning off the light, she made her way to the far side of the bed by the wall. Lukas always slept closest to the door. She laid down and pulled the quilt to her shoulders.

Laying still the dead silence more noticeable. No heavy breathing. Loud snores. Or footsteps from above. She really was all alone. Claire closed her eyes willing herself to fall asleep. Exhaustion took over and within minutes, she had drifted to sleep.

David sat at the table with the Murphy's. He was lucky he made it back in time for her meat pie.

"Good pie, Betsy!" Mr. Murphy said wiping his mouth with his napkin.

"Yum," David added.

"Than' ye!" Mrs. Murphy beamed with pride as she lifted her filled spoon to her mouth. She looked over the piece. The crust flaky, the filling just the right texture. Her meat pie had won blue ribbons at the state fair and this one was no difference. She covered the spoon with her mouth. It is delicious!

When David finished, he thanked Mrs. Murphy for the meal and retreated to his room in the barn. He sat down on his bed. He thought about his friend Jacob and what faced him. *I remember that night well.*

* * * * * * * * *

Alone in his dimly lit room in Highland Park, a young man sat in an upholstered chair by the window. In his right hand, the tiny glow of his cigarette. He lifted his hand to his mouth and inhaled. The glow brightened.

The events of last year weighted heavy on his soul. *What did I do? Why?* He thought as he raked his left hand through his sandy blonde hair. He wondered his family. He wasn't sure where they were living today. Their last letter, two years ago, said they had settled in Colorado. The Denver area. He wondered what his mama would say about his actions. Or if he could ever forgive himself.

CHAPTER 9

At the hospital, Lillian climbed the staircase; her arms loaded down with several pieces of wood. It was her third trip, and it tired her arms. This should be enough to last the night! At the top of the stairs, she turned to walk towards her ward.

"How many trips have you made?" another nursing student asked as she walked away.

Lillian turned to find the other nurse on her way down the steps and said, "It's my third. And you?"

"Three for me too."

Lillian walked into the ward and stacked the wood by the fireplace. She brushed the dirt and splinters from her white uniform. Then turned and walked between the beds to check her patients. They were all sound asleep.

Except for one. Her Papa laid awake, his eyes wide open staring at the ceiling.

"Papa," Lillian said as she sat in the chair next to him. She reached for his hand. Grasping it gently, she asked, "Papa, how are you feeling?"

He didn't respond.

"Papa, it's Lillian. You are at the hospital. Do you remember why?"

Still nothing. He doesn't want to talk. Or can't, Dr. Baker said he didn't know what was wrong with him.

"Papa, please squeeze my hand if you can hear me."

Lillian waited a minute before she repeated, "Papa, please squeeze my hand."

Knowing what a stubborn old man her father was, Lillian finally added, "Papa, if you don't squeeze my hand, Doc Baker is not goin' to let ya go home."

Lillian felt pressure on her hand.

"Yes, Papa, yes! You are at the hospital. Do you know why? Squeeze my hand."

When she felt nothing, Lillian added, "Papa, they found you in the stable. On the ground. You have no injuries. Do you hurt anywhere?"

"Dr. Baker examined you. Do you remember what happened yesterday? Do you remember what yesterday was?"

Lillian watched as her father's eyes filled with tears. The tears ran out of the corners of his eyes and down the sides of his face.

"You remember?"

He squeezed her hand.

* * * * * * * * *

April 14, 1903

Jacob awoken to the sounds of footsteps and muffled voices above him. He didn't think he would be able to sleep last night but after tossing and turning for hours, fatigue creeped in and he slept the rest of the night. He laid there for a few minutes and wondered what time they would take him to court.

His stomach growled. He hoped that they would bring him breakfast, but his stomach knotted up when he thought about spending another night in jail. Jacob heard someone coming down the steps. He sat up.

"My, my, my! As I live and breathe, Jacob Johansson. I did not believe all the gossip 'bout you." Jacob looked up and saw Adelaide Landers. Her long blonde hair pulled up with a bun in her hair. Curly strands escaped the bun and framed her face. Her bright colored dresses replaced with a simple black skirt and white blouse. She looked grown up but still as pretty as the last time he saw her. She stood at the bottom of the stairs and smiling, she held a tray in her hands in front of her. The contents covered with a cloth napkin. His breakfast.

"I did not believe them when I heard it was you in here."

"Hello, Adelaide," Jacob smiled sheepishly.

"G'morning, Jacob," she said in her sweet twangy voice.

Jacob stood up and walked to the jail door.

"Aren't you a welcome sight? Pretty as ever," he said with a smile. He hadn't seen her since her brother's trial last month. "Surprised to see you delivering my breakfast. Why aren't you in school?"

"I don't go anymore. I had to find work to help my mother out. Tom's trial cost a lot of money." She said before adding, "I probably shouldn't have said that. I work at the restaurant two blocks south of the trolley stop in Oakland. We deliver the breakfasts whenever there is a prisoner. Water's Restaurant brings dinner and supper."

She held up the tray of food, then crouched down and pushed it under the bars.

"Officer O'Reilly will take your tray when you are finished."

Adelaide turned to walk away.

"Adelaide? It was sure nice seeing your pretty face."

Adelaide turned back to look at Jacob.

"Oh, Jacob. I thought you were betrothed."

"Nah, I ain't BE-trothed or anything. Besides, I am just calling it as I see it."

"Why, Jacob Johansson, even behind bars you are a charmer!" she said with a flirty smile. "And Jacob,"

"Yea."

"When you get out of here, stop in the diner. I work the breakfast and dinner shifts." Then she turned and disappeared up the steps.

Jacob stared as she disappeared up the steps before he bent down to pick up the tray and carried it to the bench. He uncovered the food. Eggs, ham, and biscuits with gravy. Jacob grabbed the fork and dug it into the biscuits and gravy.

"Hmmm," he said as he lowered the utensil to scoop up the eggs. He quickly cleared the fork and dug in for another bite. Within minutes, the plate was empty. Jacob wiped his mouth with the cloth napkin and laid it down on the tray. He didn't realize he was that hungry.

He picked up the cup of coffee and took a sip. The robust flavor awakened his senses. The last twenty-four hours were just a blur.

Above him, more footsteps, and voices. The steps moved above him. It was more than one person. Detective and Police Chief. They were coming to get him to take him downtown.

His instincts were correct. Detective Maloney appeared at the bottom of the stairs followed by the Police Chief.

"We will take you downtown now," Detective Maloney said.

Jacob stood up. Detective Maloney unlocked the cell and opened the door for Jacob to exit.

Jacob followed the detective up the stairs. The police chief behind him. They escorted him to the back door where the paddy wagon awaited. Another officer sat behind the reins.

Jacob climbed into the back. He heard the door lock. Jacob sat on the bench and prepared for a bumpy ride.

After thirty minutes of bouncing the wagon came to a halt. He peered out the window and watched two state policemen walk towards the wagon.

They opened the back door, and the officer addressed him.

"James Jacob Johansson?"

"Yeah."

"Step out of the wagon."

Jacob obeyed and stepped down on to the stone walkway. Flanking him, the officers held his upper arm and directed him inside the courtroom.

They took him to the holding cell. Inside, three barred cells sat along one wall. Other prisoners had already arrived and were sitting on the benches awaiting their fate.

They directed Jacob to the middle cell. They unlocked the gate and nudged him to enter.

Jacob entered and sat down on the bench.

"Whacha in for?" a gruffly man asked.

"Uh, they say I killed my siblings."

"Oh, yeah. Public intoxication for me. My wife ain't going to be happy 'bout this. Second time this year. Ya married?"

"Uh, nah. I am courting' a girl." Or I was. Not sure her father will like this.

"Didja do it?"

"What? What kind of question is that?"

"Just asking."

Jacob turned away from the man. What is takin' them so long, Jacob thought. It had only been a few minutes but seemed like ages to him.

Finally, the door opened. The officers stepped in. One officer looked down at the paper in his hand and yelled out, "Kennedy, Johnson, O'Boyle. Step to the front of the cell."

Three men including Jacob's cellmate stood up. The second officer unlocked each cell and the men followed them out of the room. The door closed leaving Jacob and a few other men to wait their turn.

"They take the intoxication cases first. Me and that guy are in for robbery. Said we stole chickens. What are you in for?"

"Murder," Jacob replied. The man's mouth dropped. That ought to shut them up, Jacob thought, tired of small talk, so he said nothing else. He turned to look the other way to avoid any more questions.

* * * * * * * * *

Lillian sat at the table in the ward. It was barely six in the morning. The sun had risen and peering through the curtains. The men in her ward awakened. Soon, the day nurse would relieve her.

Lillian stood up and walked towards the large window. She raised her arms and pulled the curtain panels to the sides allowing the bright sun to light up the room. She moved to the other window and did the same thing.

"Why ya doing that?" the old patient yelled covering his eyes with his hands.

"Oh, Mr. Nilsson. Just trying to brighten up the place."

"Your smile does that."

Lillian laughed to herself. He says that to all the nurses. She walked down the row of beds checking the patients as she passed them. She stopped in front of her own father.

"Papa how are you feeling this morning?"

For the first time in a day, Lukas moved. Using his arms, he sat up in bed.

"Better," he replied.

Lillian sighed and smiled. Mama will be so happy when she gets here. She walked over to her father and leaned down to plant a kiss on his forehead.

"My shift is over soon. Another nurse will serve breakfast. I must get my rest."

He nodded. As she walked away, he said, "Thank ya." Lillian's bottom lip quivered. She thought she would burst into tears when the day nurse arrives. Lillian quickly ran out into the hallway and cried.

"Is it your papa?" the nurse asked as she followed her out into the hallway. She was on duty when they admitted him yesterday.

"My papa sat up and spoke. Finally."

"Oh, Lillian," she said as she put her arm around her shoulder. "You must go rest now. I will give him the best of care."

"Yes, thank you."

Lillian started towards the stairs. At the bottom of the steps, she ran into Dr. Baker. He could see she had been crying.

"Is something wrong with Lukas?"

"No, these are happy tears. He sat up in bed and he spoke."

"He did. That's great!" Dr. Baker exclaimed. "But that still leaves me wondering what was wrong with him?"

"Yesterday was the first anniversary of Gracie and Timmy's death."

"Hmmm," he said running two fingers and his thumb around his chin.

"I must rest before my class this afternoon and Mama arrives."

"I will go examine him. If everything checks out, I think he can go home today."

Lillian walked out the door and turned towards the nurses living quarters.

"Lil! Lil!" She recognized that voice and turned around.

"Benjamin! Are you starting your shift?"

Benjamin Carpenter reached Lillian and took her hand. "Yes, I couldn't start my rounds without seeing you first."

"My papa sat up. He spoke this morning. He didn't say much, but he spoke. Do you know what this means? He is not sick. Not sick."

"That's wonderful news! We still have to examine him first."

"He will probably go home today, will he not?"

"My studies, medical studies suggest there must be something that ails him."

"Dr. Baker will examine him again. Remember, I told you about my brother and sister's murder. It was one year ago yesterday."

"Oh! Hmmm. That could explain..." Benjamin looked up as he thought for a minute. His mind raced as he recalled lectures and class assignments.

"What?"

"I recall from my studies last year. We studied about the insane."

"My papa isn't batty, Benjamin! Don't you say that! He is not insane," Lillian said as she clenched her fists.

"Not insane to admit to an asylum. He was so distraught it paralyzed him. It's called melancholia. Last night, I read about it in my textbook. Either that or he had dropsy. But you said he was better this morning, so it rules that out."

"Could it have been a mild case?"

"We will see if he lost any motor skills when we examine him."

"You better run. Dr. Baker was on his way up there just a few minutes ago."

"Get some rest! Bye, my beautiful Lily!"

Lillian smiled and ran up the steps of the nurse's home. She needed a few hours' sleep before her afternoon class. In her room, she removed her uniform, closed the curtains, and climbed under the quilt. She didn't bother to change into her nightgown. Lillian fell asleep at once.

* * * * * * * * * *

John rose before dawn. He wanted to finish his chores before he received the call from the attorney. He quietly dressed not wanting to awake either Emma or Timmy. He stopped by the cradle that sat at the foot of their bed for just a few seconds and listened to the soft breathing sounds. His little boy sound sleep; his fingers close to his mouth. He turned back to watch his wife sleeping. She needed plenty of rest now. His son moved. John crept out of the room. He listened for a few minutes to make sure he hadn't disturbed either of them. He knew Emma only had a few more minutes of sleep before their little boy would call for his mama.

He opened the back door and slipped out quietly closing the door behind him. His first stop was the barn to milk his cows. He wasted no time talking to them; just grabbed his stool and bucket. He milked the first cow. His thoughts drifted to Jacob. He wondered what went through his mind when Jacob woke that morning. He silently prayed for his brother.

Once the bucket was full, he dumped it into the canister and moved to the next cow. He finished in record time. He quickly fed the cattle and the cats that roamed the barn. He carried the canister to the spring house before heading to the chicken coop. He fed the hens and retrieved the eggs. He placed the eggs in a basket by the door.

Now that the cattle had eaten, he herded them out to the pasture. He retrieved the egg basket and carried them into the

102

house. Fresh eggs for breakfast.

John opened the door and entered the kitchen. The smell of bacon filled the air. On the stove, the meat in a cast-iron skillet sizzled sending its aroma into the air.

At the kitchen table, he found Emma and his baby boy. Timmy sat in his high chair. With his blonde curly hair and chubby cheeks, he reminded him of the cherubs from picture books. He yanked at the bib around his neck as Emma tried to feed him, but his son wanted nothing to do with oatmeal that morning. Instead, he closed his mouth tightly and shook his head. They both looked up when John closed the door.

"Eh. Eh." Timmy chirped reaching his arm towards his father.

"I don't know if he is happy to see me or the basket of eggs."

"The eggs, sorry to say."

Emma dropped the spoon in its bowl and pushed it away from her son. "This boy is not having anything to do with the porridge. I give up. He won't eat anything but eggs."

He handed the basket to Emma and kissed his wife on the cheek. John said, "It's a good thing we have a dozen this morning. Did you sleep well? How are you feeling?"

"Yes, I did. I am refreshed. I could clean all the windows!" She turned on the stove and added lard to the cast-iron skillet on the burner.

"But you won't!" John said firmly as he remembered her last pregnancy. Her pregnancy took over her tiny frame and forced her into bedrest for the last two months of her pregnancy.

"No, I won't. I have laundry today. I will wash the baby things. As rough and tough as this little boy is, there's plenty of mending to do. I only have another three months until this one arrives." Emma rested her hands on her protruding belly. "Hopefully, he will take a long nap or two today." Emma lovingly patted her boy's head.

"As soon as I hear from the attorney, I will leave. I hate to leave you again today. I don't think I will be gone all day again. I need to check on my father too."

"I will be fine. My mama is just down the road. And Jimmy will be here. Please send my love to your mother and father. And Jacob too. I pray that this is all resolved."

"I will. If I knew how long it took, I would take this little man with me," John said as he lifted the tray and scooped his son out of the chair. He swung him up to the ceiling; Timmy giggled with joy.

"He's a tough little boy," Emma chimed in. Emma cracked a couple eggs over her cast iron pan.

"Why don't I take him?" John asked. "I'm sure my mother would love to see him."

"If you think it will be all right. I will pack you a lunch and clean nappies."

John turned and winced. He had forgotten about changing his nappies. *Mama would not mind changing them!*

Emma flip over the eggs. She grabbed a plate from the shelf and carefully removed the fried eggs. She placed a few slices of bacon next to the eggs.

Placing it down in front of her husband, she said, "Fresh biscuits in the basket in front of you."

She scooped out another egg and placed in a small bowl. Last, she made a plate for herself. She poured coffee into two cups and gave one to her husband. Next, she filled a metal cup with milk for her son.

She sat down at the table and spooned up eggs for her son. He gobbled up the eggs right away and whined for more. In between, Emma tried to feed herself.

After they had finished, she quickly washed the dishes as her son sat on the floor at her feet. Between his legs, a set of wooden blocks, Emma's father made for him. Timmy picked up a block and placed it on another block. He waved his tiny hand at the blocks and knocked them down. Emma proudly watched him with his new trick. She was in awe over his daily accomplishments. She adored her son and could watch him for hours.

When she had done cleaning in the breakfast dishes and pans, she scooped up her boy and carried him into the bedroom. With him resting on her hip, she picked up two neatly folded diapers. The bucket in the corner already full of the dirty ones. All I do is wash diapers. With a second baby, there will be twice as many. "Oh, but I wouldn't trade my life for mounds of gold. I love you so much!" Emma kissed little Timmy's pudgy cheek.

She sat him on the bed and lowered herself down next to him. His white short gown barely covered his chubby legs. She held his hands as he tried to stand. Once he was standing, he giggled, wiggled, and fell back down with a plop. They both laughed together.

John watched them from the door for a minute before

announcing himself.

"I need to check the fields. Your brother is in the barn fixing the plow. If the attorney telephones, send him to get me."

"I will."

CHAPTER 10

Claire awakened with the sun. She quickly removed her nightgown. Claire slipped her arms into her shirt and buttoned it before she put on her skirt. She pinned her hair in a bun on top of her head. Before she left the room, she picked up her Bible and got down on her knees. She paged through until she found the verse she wanted. Her lips moved as she read it. When she had finished, she closed it, held it to her chest and clasp her hands to pray.

When she finished, she stood up and left the room for the kitchen. She didn't feel like eating, but decided she better eat something. She needed to stay healthy for the sake of Lukas. And Jacob. For everyone.

Claire fixed herself a cup of tea and sat down in her chair. In front of her, the basket held sweet treats, biscuits, and apple bread. Claire pulled the basket closer and peered under the cloth napkin. She pondered the selections for a minute before choosing the apple bread.

Claire broke off a corner of the bread and ate it. It tasted delicious. She finished the apple bread and drank her tea. When she finished, she quickly rinsed her teacup and placed on the drainer.

"I wish we had a telephone. I'm putting my foot down and telling Lukas we must have one." We needed one yesterday and I need one today, Claire thought to herself.

She didn't know if she should wait a few hours or walk to the hospital. It will take her a good hour to get there. She didn't want to rush Dr. Baker, especially if Lukas needed to stay longer.

"What should I do? What should I do?" Claire pondered.

Claire stood in the kitchen and looked around. "I will do laundry. That should keep me busy for hours."

Unlike her daughters, Claire didn't have a machine. She still used a washboard and a large barrel. And plenty of muscle.

Claire picked up her washboard, gathered the dirty clothes and went outside. The morning air still cool but it would be much warmer later. For the next few hours, Claire washed the clothes. First, she dipped the clothing into the soapy water, then rubbed it against the washboard. She placed the clean wet clothes on a small table.

When she finished washing the clothes, she dumped the barrel and refilled it with clean water. She rinsed each item several times then twisted to wring out the water. She hung the clothing on the line.

She finished just as her neighbor, Joe pulled up in his wagon. "Mrs. Johansson, have you any news from the hospital?"

"No, I haven't. I will go there this afternoon."

"And Gertrude thanks for the fresh milk. You are so kind."

"I am happy to share with you. You were so kind to help me yesterday. With just Lukas and I living here, we will always have more than we need, I want you to stop by and pick up another cannister when you need more milk. You have so many mouths to feed."

* * * * * * * *

Meanwhile, Jacob sat alone in the cell room. The other two men left over an hour ago. Suddenly, the door opened. Jacob looked up expecting the two court officers, but a robust well-dressed man walked in instead.

"Jacob, Robert Hammil, I am your attorney. Hired by your brother, er," he struggled to remember his brother's name. "John. I wanted to tell you about the arraignment. The judge will ask for your plea."

"My plea?"

"Yes, it's guilty or not guilty. They are your only choices. And you will say?"

"Not guilty. I'm not guilty." *I think I am not guilty. I don't remember that night*, he thought. He wondered if he should tell the attorney he remembered nothing about that night.

"Good, good. Then the judge will decide your bail. The district attorney will argue one thousand." Jacob's mouth dropped open. "Oh, no, I'll argue for two hundred and fifty dollars. That way the judge will say five hundred. At the most, he might go up to seven hundred and fifty. I will telephone your brother and he will bring the bail money. It could take him an hour or more to get here. You and I will meet to discuss the trial. You should be released early afternoon."

"What time is it now?" Jacob asked.

"About ten thirty."

Jacob nodded. He had lost track of time.

Jacob and the attorney chatted for a few more minutes. Mostly, for the attorney's sake; he needed to get to know Jacob for the hearing. He asked questions about his job, his farm, his plans. The time passed quickly.

When the door opened, they both stood. Jacob's felt a knot in the pit of his stomach, his palms sweat, and his heart raced, he was nervous. He followed the court officers out of the room and down the hall. His attorney walked behind them.

They opened the door to the courtroom. Inside, the judge sat at his desk. A court reporter in front of him. A bailiff stood on the other side.

"James Jacob Johansson," the bailiff said as he handed the arrest warrant to the judge.

The judge read the warrant and placed it down on the desk in front of him. "Mr. Johansson, I charge you the murders of Grace Johansson and Timothy Johansson, how do you plead?"

Jacob spoke but his voice cracked. He cleared his throat then said, "Not guilty, Your Honor."

The judge looked at the District Attorney Culligan. Culligan said, "The defendant is charged with the brutal murder of his own sister and brother. We are asking for the court to set the bail at one thousand dollars."

The judge nodded then looked over at Jacob's attorney.

"Your honor," he began, "The defendant is a farmer and delivers for the creamery two days a week. We request a fair and equitable bail to be, say, two-hundred and fifty dollars."

"Your honor, this was a brutal murder. That is outrageous."

The judge looked down at the warrant in front of him. After a minute or two, he looked up. He picked up his gavel and slammed it down. "I set the bail at five hundred dollars."

With that, the judge stood and disappeared into his chambers.

"I will telephone your brother right away."

The court officers walked up to Jacob. They escorted him back to the holding cell to await transport to the county jail across the road.

* * * * * * * *

Ring-ring!

Emma stopped washing the clothes and answered it. Placing the earpiece to her ear, she raised up on her tiptoes and spoke into the mouthpiece, "Hello."

"Mrs. Johansson, this is Attorney Robert Hammil. I need to speak to your husband."

"He's out in the field but if you tell me what you know, I will send a message to him."

"Tell him bail is five hundred dollars. He needs to bring the cash to the courthouse downtown. Got that?"

"Yes, I do."

"Thank you. Goodbye."

Emma said goodbye, but he had hung up. She ran out of the house towards the barn where her brother worked on the plow.

"Jimmy, the attorney called," Emma panted. Running in her condition took her breath away. She held one hand under her belly for support.

Jimmy dropped his tools and stood up.

"That's the message."

"Tell him the bail is five hundred, and he needs to take it to the courthouse downtown."

"Got it," he said as he raced out of the barn.

Emma ran back to the house. If John was taking Timmy with him, she needed to finish packing his bag. Emma peeked into the bassinet where baby Timmy slept. His angelic face melted her heart.

The thought of an entire day without him broke her heart. At just seven months old, her whole life revolved around him. Always just a few feet away from her, sitting in a walker or on the floor by her feet.

Emma suddenly stood up.

I will go with them!

By the time, John returned from the fields, Emma was ready to go. The baby buggy and a bag filled with diapers sat side by side on the kitchen floor. Emma's shawl wrapped around her shoulders barely covered her protruding belly; baby Timmy asleep in the small straw bassinet on the floor beside her.

"Where are you going?"

"I'm coming with you. I haven't been to town in months. We can visit with Chloe or Anna Belle while you go downtown."

He should tell her all the reasons she should stay home, but he knew his wife wouldn't back down, so he reluctantly agreed. He shook his head and said, "If you insist, we must stop to see mama too. If she heard, we were in Highland Park and didn't stop; we would never hear the end. With the Landers kid's trial, she hasn't seen Timmy in months."

John picked up the buggy and carried outside. He placed it in the wagon. He retrieved the bassinet with his son sound asleep.

Emma followed as she tied the bow to her hat under her chin.

"Do ya wanna to sit up front with me or back here?"

"I will seat in back with Timmy. In case he wakes."

John removed a box step and placed on the ground. With one hand on the side of the wagon, John helped her into the wagon. A bench sat across one side. Emma sat down close to the bassinet. John climbed up front and they left for town. His wallet with the money in the breast pocket of his coat.

Emma watched her son sleep; the rocking of the wagon made her sleepy. She rested her head against the back of the bench and closed her eyes. As she drifted off to sleep, she listened to the melodic sounds of her husband's whistling, the gravel under the wagon wheels, and the sound of the leaves rustling in the wind.

A half hour later, John slowed down the wagon. The wagon jerked, and Emma woke. She opened her eyes and looked at the surroundings. "We'll stop at the farm first to see Mama." Emma nodded in agreement.

John turned the wagon on to Madison Avenue. They passed the knoll where his siblings were killed. The grass in the ditches grew tall. The gravel no longer showed drag marks. The crude crosses gone. *It is as if nothing happened here*, Emma thought.

John steered the wagon to the back of the house stopping just before the water pump. John jumped down from the wagon. He walked around the back and said, "Wait here. I want to see if Mama is home."

Emma smiled and looked around him. John turned to see his mother walking towards them.

"John! Emma! What brings you here?"

John hugged his mother and kissed her cheek. "I'm on my way downtown to pay the bail for Jacob. Emma insisted on coming with us. Thought we would stop here first."

"Please come inside. I want to see my grandson. I want to hold him and kiss his cheeks," she cooed.

John helped Emma out of the wagon, then climbed in to retrieve Timmy. He handed the basket down to his mother. They jumped to the ground. He took the handle from his mother and carried it into the house. His mother and Emma walked ahead of him. Claire had her arm around Emma as they walked inside. Emma planted herself in a chair at the table; his mother placed the teapot on the stove.

"Are you hungry? I have biscuits and apple bread."

"Yes, please. How is Papa? What have you heard from the hospital?"

"Yes. Better news. Dr. Baker sent a message. Your papa sat up and spoke. He's back to his gruff old self. He can't go home until this afternoon."

"Do they know what was wrong with him?"

"They don't know or didn't want to say."

"Mama, did they say he had his gun?" Emma asked.

"It was in the barn from earlier. He wanted to shoot a fox that was getting into the chicken coop and killing our flock."

Claire didn't want to even think of Lukas killing himself. She continued changing the subject, "I can promise you this, we will have a telephone in this house."

John laughed. His mother has wanted a telephone when their neighbors installed theirs. He knew how much his father resisted new inventions. He balked at adding electricity, indoor plumbing, or a privy under the stairs but always gave in to his mother. At the same time, he liked turning a switch for light or not having to go out in the middle of the night to use the outhouse.

"I like having a telephone," Emma piped in. "If John hadn't called when he found out about Jacob yesterday, I would have worried all day."

"The attorney I hired called mid-morning. Jacob's bail is five hundred dollars. We can't stay long. I want to drop Emma and the baby off at Chloe's."

Timmy stirred. His eyes opened and so did his mouth. He screamed at the top of his lungs.

"Oh, my! He's probably hungry." Emma quickly picked him up and held him tightly. She stood up, patted his back, and swayed back and forth as she sweetly hummed to settle him down. When he stopped crying, she held him up and looked into his eyes and said, "Is mama's baby hungry?"

"Emma, you can use our bedroom."

Emma thanked her and left to nurse her baby; leaving John and his mother alone to talk.

"The cows. Do I need to milk the cows?" John remembered that Jacob still milked the cows both morning and night even though he had his own farm to tend.

"No, our hired hand came this morning, milked them and they are out in the pasture. He's in the fields plowing now."

"Good."

"The neighbor milked them last night. I gave them a canister of milk for his troubles. He has so many mouths to feed."

"With another one due soon too." Jacob concerned for his mother's health said, "Mama, did you sleep last night? You look tired."

"I went to bed early. I fell asleep right away."

"It worries me to see you like this."

"I believe God is testing my faith," she said, then changed the subject "How is Emma feeling this time?"

"She's says fine, but Timmy is a handful. Every day, he's doing something new. Pulling himself up, crawling, he keeps her on her toes. She falls asleep the minute her head touches the pillow."

Claire smiled.

"What?"

"Oh, John, your son is just like you. He is his father's son."

"He will be barely ten months old when the second one is due to arrive. I hope Emma is ready for two babies."

"John, Chloe and Jacob are less than a year apart and I had you too. Her maternal instincts will help her."

At the mention of Jacob's name, John stood up and looked towards the closed door, "If I'm going to stop at Chloe's, I need to be on my way."

"She will be in the bedroom awhile. Why don't you go? They can stay with me,"

"Uh. I don't know, Mama. Timmy can be a handful." John didn't want to burden his mama.

"I will talk to her," Claire stood and walked to the closed door. She rapped quietly and said, "Emma, may I come in?"

Claire opened the door and walked in closing the door behind her. John finished his tea and reached for a sweet treat. He broke off a piece of the apple bread and dropped it in his mouth. It was delicious.

Mama sure makes the best apple bread. Mmm-mmm.

The closed door opened, and Claire reentered the kitchen. "John, they will stay with me. Dr. Baker says I should come to the hospital but not until late this afternoon. And baby Timmy has grown so much since the last time I saw him. Emma can rest while I watch him."

"Are you sure?"

"Yes, now run along and get your brother out of jail." Claire quickly added as John headed towards the door, "John, tell Jacob I love him."

"I will. I'll be back quickly," John said as he left the house. A few minutes later, Claire heard the wagon pulling away. She looked out the window and saw the buggy sitting by the water pump. *Wonderful! I can take baby Timmy for a walk while Emma rests,* Claire thought smiling to herself.

CHAPTER 11

John skipped the trolley and steered the wagon downtown. He needed to hurry. He had to bail out Jacob, take him to Chloe's and back to the farm to get Emma and the baby. He knew he should give his mother a lift to the hospital.

John pulled his wagon to the side of the courthouse. He tied the reins to the post and ran to the front door. Inside, an officer sat in front of a desk. The newspaper spread across it. Behind him, massive steps showed the way to the second floor and the courtrooms.

The officer looked up when he heard John's footsteps. "Can I help you?"

"Ah, yea, um, where do I go to pay bail for my, someone?"

"Down the hall. First door on the left."

John thanked him and hurried down the hall. When he reached the door, he hesitated. He wasn't sure if he should knock first or just walk in. He walked in.

Inside, a wall with two openings split the room in half. John thought it resembled a bank. A bald man sat in one window. His jacket hung in the corner on a coat tree. The sleeves of his shirt rolled up and exposed his forearms. His ear held an extra pencil. A funny-looking machine in front of him. The man pushed down on the buttons, then pulled the lever. He repeated the step another time before he looked up.

"Can I help you?"

"Is this where I pay bail?"

"This is the place. Whose bail are you paying?"

"Jac, James Johansson," John corrected it to his brother's legal name.

The man opened a leather book in front of him. Using his finger, he scanned the page. About halfway down the page, he stopped and looked up. "Five hundred dollars."

John pulled his wallet out of his front pocked and opened it to take out the money. He counted the money before handing it to the man.

"Five hundred dollars," he said.

The man counted out the money and wrote something in his book. He filled out the release papers and handed it to John. "You need to give that to the jail officer. I will telephone the jail to let them know you are coming to get the prisoner." He stood up and walked to the phone in the corner. He lifted the earpiece and spoke into the phone.

"Operator, can you connect me to the jail?"

The man turned and looked at John. "Just a minute."

"Kennedy. Potter here. Someone paid the bail on Johansson. He can be released now. I will send him over."

He hung up the phone.

"You need to go to the county jail. It's the building across the street."

"Thank you," John said as he turned to leave the room.

Outside, John looked at the surrounding buildings. One building had bars on the windows. That must be it.

John walked to the building and climbed the two steps to the door. He opened the door and stepped inside. John looked around the room. Directly in front him, an officer sat at a desk reading the newspaper. Behind him, metal bars spanned from floor to ceiling.

More bars, he thought. The officer looked up from his paper and acknowledged John.

"You here for Johansson?" he asked.

"Yea." John handed him the signed paper from the court clerk.

The officer took the paper from John and scanned the document.

"Everything is in order." The officer stood up. He walked over the door, unlocked it and stepped behind the barred wall. He disappeared down the hall leaving John standing there. A few minutes later, he returned and said, "he will be out in a few minutes. You can take a seat while you are waiting."

John looked to either side of him. A long bench sat across one wall with a newspaper scattered across it. John picked up the paper and sat down. He wondered how long it would take.

Miles away at the farm, Emma and Claire enjoyed their dinner. With his belly full, baby Timmy quietly played with his blocks and babbled to himself. This allowed his mother and grandmother to visit.

"How are you feeling?" Claire asked Emma. In their short visit, she could see that Timmy was a handful.

"Tired! This little man keeps me busy."

"Why don't you lay down? And I will take him for a walk. John left the buggy."

"I hate to impose."

"You won't be. I don't get to spend much time with my grandson and would love to take care of him," Claire replied as she reached down to touch his cheek.

Baby Timmy giggled.

"If you don't mind. A short nap will be nice. I didn't sleep well last night."

"It is a bit dusty but why don't you go upstairs to the girls' room?"

"Yes, I will do that. Thank you."

Emma left the room. Claire wrapped her shawl around her shoulders before she picked up her grandson. She put on his hat and grabbed his blanket.

Outside, she placed him in his buggy and tucked his blanket around him. She walked down to the street and turned towards Poor Farm Road. The other direction would take it past the spot where her children's life ended so brutally. Even a year later, Claire avoided going that way. It made for longer trips when visiting Eliza Davis or other neighbors. She hoped that someday, she could venture by that site but today wasn't the day.

"I will let your mama rest for an hour," she said to her smiling grandson. He sat in the buggy, his tiny hands held on to the sides, his wide brown eyes looked from side to side, his blonde hair peeked out from under his hat.

A bird flew above them. Baby Timmy raised his arm to the sky.

"Yes, I see the bird."

That scene played again as bird after bird flew by. Claire laughed and marveled at how alert he was.

As they walked along the gravel road, the buggy bounced and rocked back and forth. Timmy yawned. His eyes heavy as he fought to keep them open. His head dropped as he drifted to sleep but he would wake up right away and lift his head. Claire laughed each time and wondered how many times it would take before he fell asleep. Unable to fight it any longer, Timmy finally succumbed to the rocking of the buggy.

Claire stopped the buggy and gently laid her grandson down. She covered him with the blanket, ran her finger across his chubby cheek and hoped Lukas would heal so he could enjoy their ever-growing family. In four weeks, Anna Belle's baby would arrive. Chloe and Emma's just a few months later.

Claire turned around and headed back home. By the time they arrive back at the farm, it will be two o'clock.

CHAPTER 12

Earlier, Dr. Baker went directly to see Lukas. As he entered the ward, the sight of Lukas sitting up in bed both surprised and mystified him. He sat there eating breakfast like nothing happened. Lukas' inability to move his limbs or speak yesterday baffled him. Yesterday, the symptoms convince the doctor he suffered a stroke. His recovery pointed to something else. But what?

The ward nurse walked over to greet the doctor.

"Are you here to see Mr. Johansson?"

"Yes, I am. Is there a wheelchair available?" he asked looking around the room.

"Yes, there's one in the corner behind that curtain over there," she replied pointing to the drawn curtains. "Shall I retrieve it for you?"

"Yes, please," he responded as he walked away.

"Ven can I get out of here?" Lukas barked when Dr. Baker reached him.

"We need to examine you again."

"I'm good," he said as he tried to get out of bed.

Dr. Baker stopped him. 'Lukas, we need you to take it easy. Until we figure out what is wrong."

The ward nurse arrived with the wheelchair as he finished his statement.

"I will take you to the examination room. Dr. Carpenter will assist," he said wondering if Lukas recognized his daughter's fiancé's name.

"Now, let me help you up and in this wheelchair."

"I ain't no invalid. I can valk."

"Until we determine what is wrong with you, you need to let me push you." Dr. Baker repeated his earlier comments. He sure is a stubborn old grouse.

Dr. Baker reached out and wrapped his hand around Lukas' forearm. Lukas tried to shake him off.

"I need no help."

Dr. Baker didn't want to argue with him, so he said, "Lukas, if you want to go home, you need to listen to me."

Lukas stopped resisting and let him help. Once seated, Dr. Baker pushed the wheelchair down the room towards the door. He wheeled him to the last room at the end of the hall.

By now, Dr. Carpenter was waiting. A white coat covered his street clothes, the stethoscope hung loosely around his neck. He held a leather-covered book in his hands.

"I trust you know Dr. Carpenter."

"Huh? Vat?"

"You HAVE met Dr. Carpenter, haven't you?" Dr. Baker knew they have met since Benjamin approached Lukas before he courted her and then again, when he asked for her hand in marriage.

Although, marriage was more than a year away. As a student, Lillian couldn't marry until her formal studies completed. Benjamin had one more year left before he could practice medicine. Once he graduated, he would set up practice in one of the many small but growing towns in central Iowa. He had heard of several that didn't have a full-time doctor in town and residents forced to travel to the next town for their medical needs.

"Ja, ja. I've met him," Lukas replied when he wasn't sure where.

Dr. Baker stopped the wheelchair by the examination table. He held the chair as Lukas pushed himself out. Lukas sat on the edge of the table.

Drs. Baker and Carpenter began their exam. They listened to his heart and lungs, checked his ears, eyes and throat, and performed the knee jerk test. He had Lukas lay down, asked him to lift his legs and hands, and push on the doctor's hand as hard as he could. They repeated this with all limbs.

Dr. Baker shook his head. He could find nothing physically wrong with him.

He signaled for Dr. Carpenter to follow him out into the hall. Outside, Dr. Baker said, "He's passed all the tests. If he had a stroke, the knee jerk would have showed it. Everything is normal. Do you concur, Doctor?"

"Yes, I do," he said. "Um, er."

"What is it?"

"I didn't want to bring this up. Last year, we studied Melancholia. Mr. Johansson, I mean, the patient has all the classic signs; Lillian says he has depressed. So, depressed they feared he would take his own life. He hasn't been himself since the deaths of his children. The death of Timmy. Lillian said he never mentions her sister. Yesterday, he had abnormal motor functions and was in a vegetative state. It wasn't until earlier today when I was reminded that it was one year ago that someone killed his son and daughter, I believe it could be melancholia."

"Interesting, hmm." Dr. Baker remembered the gun laying under Lukas' vegetated body.

"He didn't remember me. I could see it in his eyes he didn't remember who I was. Even though, I have been to the house frequently. I have sat at the same table with him for dinner and spoke with him to ask for Lillian's hand. He does not understand who I am, and I sat next to him at their house."

"I will read up on this before I say anything to Lukas. Before I can diagnose it," Dr. Baker said. "Take Lukas back to the ward. I will get word to Claire about his condition."

Dr. Carpenter regretted saying anything. This was his fiancé's father. As he turned to go back into the examination room, Dr. Baker said, "Good research, Doctor."

Dr. Carpenter smiled as he went in the room.

"I will take you back to the ward now. Can you get down or do you need help?"

"I'm not a cripple. And why aren't I going home?"

"We still don't know what is ailing you."

Lukas became angrier as his future son-in-law pushed him down the hall. He muttered under his breath, but Benjamin could still hear him.

"There's nuttin' vong with me. I need to get back to my farm. I have farming to do. I need to plow my fields. Just let me out of here."

"With all due respect, Mr. Johansson, we think there is."

Lukas mumbled, "I don't need no vippersnapper telling me vat I can or can't do. There is nuttin' vong vith me."

Benjamin smiled; thankful now he didn't recognize him.

The ward nurse greeted them. Benjamin left Lukas in her care. She steered the chair to his bed. Then she fluffed the feather pillows and offered her arm to help him into the bed. When he sat comfortably in his bed, she asked, "Is there anything you need?"

"I need to leave. I have a farm to take care of. Let me out of here."

"You know I can't do that, Mr. Johansson. Dr. Baker is the only one who can do that. I will serve supper shortly. I walked by the kitchen and it smells delicious."

Lukas pouted; his arms folded in front of him.

Just a few miles away, John patiently awaited his brother. He wished they hurried; he worried about his mama with Timmy. He knew she wanted to get to the hospital, but she couldn't pass up an opportunity to spend time with her grandson. Playing with Timmy would take her mind off of her troubles. He smiled thinking his wife knew what she was doing when she tagged along.

The sound of the bars closing brought John back to reality. He looked up to see his brother standing in front of him.

"A penny for your thoughts," Jacob said.

Not wanting any ribbing from his brother, he replied, "Just about my farm." A sheepish grin on his face.

Jacob knew he lied. He always gets that silly grin when he's not telling the truth.

The two brothers walked out of the jailhouse. Jacob stopped at the top of the steps and looked around. He took in a deep breath enjoying every minute. After over twenty-four hours in the drafty smelly cells, it felt good to be out. They walked towards John's wagon in front of the courthouse.

"Truth be told, brother, I would not blame ya if you were thinking about your wife. You did pick a good one. I can only hope that the one I marry is half as good. Heck, with my luck, I will end up with some old battle-axe." Jacob joked.

"That girl you have been courting is a real looker. Isabelle, right?"

"I don't think her father was too keen on me from the beginning, this ain't going to help me win him over."

John untied the reins and climbed into the wagon. Jacob sat next to him.

"I will take you to Chloe's for tonight. Come tomorrow, we can figure out your farm. Mama asked Daniel to take over afternoon milking."

"There is still the abutting land."

"That will take some figuring out."

Jacob nodded. He thought about selling the farm and moving outside of town. But planting season has started and there isn't a farmer in town that would buy it right now.

John snapped the reins when they left the downtown area. "I better hurry. Emma and the baby rode with me and I left them with Mama. Timmy can be a handful."

The wagon sped off. They traveled at a fast speed until they reached Highland Park area. John slowed down the horse to a trot.

"Want me to hide in back?" Jacob asked.

"Why?"

"Do you want to be seen with an accused murderer?"

"I am with my brother."

The sidewalks in Highland Park filled with people. They stopped and stared; pointed and whispered to one another but John and Jacob held their heads high and looked straight ahead.

John turned down the gravel road where Chloe lived. He stopped the wagon in front of their house. As they jumped down from the wagon, Chloe greeted them.

"Hello! I have been waiting for you," she said as she waddled over. She gave Jacob a hug. "Come inside for tea and cake."

John put his arm over her shoulders and gave her a squeeze. "I have to go. I left Emma and Timmy with mama"

"I wish I would have known. I would have walked to the farm." She missed talking to Emma. The two developed a strong bond after Chloe helped while Emma was bedridden during her final month. Chloe stood by Emma and held her hand when she gave birth to Timmy.

"I had planned on dropping them off here, but Mama insisted on watching the baby while Emma rested."

John turned to walk away. About halfway to the wagon, he heard his name.

"Hey, John," Jacob called out.

John turned towards his brother.

Jacob looked at him and said, "Thank you."

John nodded and turned around.

* * * * * * * * *

Rap-rap-rap!

Lillian woke to the sound of knocking. She climbed out of bed and opened the door.

"What time is it? Did I miss our lecture? I must have

overslept."

"You have missed nothing, not even supper. Can I come in?"

Lillian opened the door more to allow her fellow student and friend, Sarah in. Sarah sat on her bed.

Lillian picked up her uniform hanging over the chair and slipped it over her shoulders.

"Sit down, Lillian. I told you it isn't even time for supper. I have news to tell you."

Lillian sat down and said, "What? Is it my father? Has he taken ill again? He was well when I left him this morning."

"No, not your father. Although, I heard he was giving Lucinda a run for her money."

"That is my papa. Then what is it?"

"It's your brother."

"John? Jacob?"

"It was Jacob. I heard they arrested him yesterday. For murder!"

"Jacob? Murder? Who?"

"Your younger brother and sister."

"Gracie and Timmy? No, no, no!" she exclaimed as she placed her face down into the palms of her hands and cried.

She thought about the brutal beating inflicted on Gracie and Timmy. She heard rumors of cracked skulls, multiple broken bones and brain matter seeped out onto the gravel road. That the killer dragged their broken bodies to the side of the road and threw their bodies into the ditch like yesterday's garbage. She remembered their innocent faces disfigured with bruises and lacerations. The futile attempt to hide the injuries with face powder. The bruises peeked through the dusting. No, Jacob couldn't have done that, could he?

She thought how it destroyed their family. How it sent her papa plummeting into depression; so distraught he kept to himself. How she heard him blame her mother time after time for Timmy's death. She remembered her sisters' weddings; how he sat by himself while the rest of family tried to forget, for just a day, the horrific tragedy. She remembered that he didn't join their trip to meet the newest family member - his first grandchild. Although, he looks at Benjamin; she's sure he doesn't see him. And last, how she feared he might take his own life.

Lillian thought about her mama; how her faith amazed her. She wondered how her mother found the strength to rise every morning. How she still prays each morning and night and attends Sunday Service alone. How her mama tried to talk to her papa, but he ignored her. After twenty-five years of marriage, a rift now divided them.

And she thought about her siblings; how each one affected by the loss of their younger brothers and sisters. But Jacob?

Jacob did it? How could he?

"Lillian, I am sorry. But I had to tell you this news. I thought it was better you heard from me then from gossip later," Sarah said. She moved closer and put her arm around Lillian's shoulder. Lillian turned her head and cried as her friend held her.

Suddenly, the tears stopped. She raised her head, took a hankie out of her pocket, and dabbed her wet eyes.

"I don't blame you. Why didn't my mama or brother tell me yesterday? Surely, they knew when they were here."

"They worried about your papa," Sarah replied, trying to be the voice of reason.

"I am sure that papa worried them," she said as she stood up. "I better hurry and finish dressing. It is almost time for supper."

"Yes, let's go."

Lillian stood in front of the mirror dresser. She looked at her reflection and said, "I need to fix my hair."

Lillian pulled the clips out of her hair. Her long blonde hair fell to her shoulders. She picked up a wide-tooth comb and smoothed out her blonde locks. Her friend, Sarah watched in awe as Lillian parted her hair into several sections than carefully brought each end together at the top of her head. Holding her hair in her hand, she loosens her grip, then twisted it until she had a bun, then secured it with hairpins. She placed her nurse's cap on top and pinned to keep it from shifting as she moved.

Her friend asked, "Where did you learn that?"

"In one of those Harper's Weekly magazines in the parlor. It's called the Gibson or the Gibson girl."

"You must teach me."

"I will. It should have more poof. I doubt our head nurse will let me wear it that way." Lillian opened her top drawer, took out a small satin bag and said, "See this. I am collecting hairs from my brush and comb. I will pin it to my hair and will have the same hairstyle as the magazines."

"I must read about it."

As the two women left the room, Lillian added, "Woman wear makeup now. No more pinching our cheeks, they have rouge now. And not just for actresses or women that frequent taverns. I heard the department store downtown sells it."

"We must go but first you must tell me more."

Lillian explained to her fellow student how to style her hair. And for a while, Lillian forgot her troubles.

* * * * * * * * *

With just the moon to light his way, the dark-haired man walked across the freshly plowed land. His deep-set brown eyes looked at the dark farmhouse in the distance.

Good, he thought. They are in bed. But he knew they would be. It was close to ten o'clock. They would have retired with the sun.

He stopped at the water pump to wash up before he also retired. Nestled among the old house and barns, the new water pump was obvious.

A year ago, a fallen tree branch used in place of the missing handle. He originally hoped to replace only the handle, but his landlord surprised him with a new pump.

His thoughts drifted back to that cool night in April. He remembered how lucky he was to find that tree branch. That branch, thick on one end and tapered down on the other end, fit perfectly in the slots and he could wash the stains from his shirt and pants. He had washed his face and hands but without a mirror, didn't know if his face was clean.

He recalled thinking he would look for the missing handle but not now. Thankful, he didn't toss a stream or pond but still too soon to retrieve now.

Standing in his britches, he had squeezed out the excess water from his clothing. He hoped they would dry by dawn. Or just the pants. He owned a few shirts. He carried the damp clothes to his room and hung them over a chair.

He shivered in the cold room. Better make a fire, he remembered thinking.

The kindling caught fire right away. Soon, potbelly stove warmed the room. He checked his clothes. The fire would dry them by morning.

The man slipped off his pants. The same ones he wore a year ago. As a farmer, blood and dirt stained clothing was the norm.

CHAPTER 13

Claire pushed the buggy towards the back door. Timmy sound asleep. Not wanting to wake the baby, she climbed the step to the door, opened it and faintly called out, "Emma, Emma!" There was no answer.

"She must be still sleeping."

Claire sat down on the stoop and watched her grandson sleep. She smiled at the faces and funny noises he made. *He must be dreaming*, she thought. She marveled at how much he looked like John.

As she watched him, his eyes opened. Claire pounced ready to pick him up when he cried out but nothing. Timmy just smiled at her.

She sat him up in the buggy and sweetly talked to him. "Did Grandmother's little boy have a good nap? Your papa should come soon. It's such a beautiful day I hate to take you inside. Now what can I do with you." Claire looked around the yard.

A small quilt hung on the line. "I wonder if that blanket is dry."

Claire stood up, picked up Timmy and carried him to the clothesline. She balanced him on one hip as she felt the quilt. It's dry. She removed the pins that held the quilt on the line, laid it out on the ground and placed Timmy in the middle. She picked up the tin bucket that held her clothespins, dump the few remaining pins on the blanket and placed the tin down in front of him. She picked up a clothespin and dropped it into the bucket.

Plunk! Timmy giggled. Claire handed him another pin and pointed to the tin.

"Drop in the bucket, Timmy," she instructed.

Plunk! The second one hit the bottom of the tin. This time Timmy reached for another clothes pin.

"That should entertain you while I take down the clothes."

Claire stood up and removed the clothes on the line. She had almost finished when Timmy cried out, "Eh, Eh." His arms reached out in front of him. Claire turned around to see John standing there.

"He knows his papa!"

John reached down and picked up his boy. He lifted him up in the air then blew a raspberry on his belly that peeked out from his shirt. Timmy giggled and kicked his feet.

"I see why Emma is tired."

"That's my job when I am finish my farm chores. Entertain Timmy so he falls right to sleep at bedtime." John looked around and continued, "Where's Emma?"

"Still resting. We took a walk, and it was too nice to go in."

Little did they know, Emma woke up and stood at the bedroom window watching them. Her eyes beamed with love. With all the troubles this family had, she wouldn't trade one day. She loved her husband, her son, his family, and her life. An answer to all her girlhood daydreams.

Emma felt sneaky watching them, so she moved away from the window and made her way to the door. John and his mother engrossed in their conversation; but Timmy saw his mama. "Ma! Ma!" he called out.

John turned to see his pretty bride standing on the stoop. She looked rested and happy. She smiled and walked towards them. John smiled back. When she reached them, Claire asked, "Did you have a nice nap?"

Emma smiled saying, "It was wonderful. Thank you so much."

"I loved taking care of my grandson. We took a long walk, and he sat on the blanket as I took down the laundry. He learned a new game."

Timmy squirmed in his papa's arms and leaned over towards Emma as he reached to put his arms around her neck.

"Someone missed his mama!" she said as John released his hold. Timmy nuzzled his face into Emma's neck and cooed.

"Everything good at the courthouse?"

"Yes. I was telling mama. Jacob is at Chloe's. I'm not sure how he and papa can farm with their property so close. We will work out something. Tomorrow."

"Any news from the hospital?" Emma asked.

"Dr. Baker is coming by in about an hour. He has a patient to check on nearby. He will bring us back home."

"Oh. Did he say anything else?"

"No, but he said not to be alarmed."

"We have a telephone if you need me," John said. "I must take my family home. It's been a long day."

"You mean a long two days!" Claire added.

"You are right. TWO long days. But we need to go." Emma and Timmy sat on a bench by the house.

They said their goodbyes. Claire held Timmy close to her. She nuzzled her face into his belly, and he giggled. John loaded the baby buggy into the wagon and brought the bassinet out from inside. This time Timmy sat in it with his blocks in front of him. Emma hugged Claire and climbed in the back again. John leaned down and kissed his mother's cheek.

"Good-bye, mama!"

"Bye. Please bring Emma and Timmy back soon. Oh, how I wish you lived closer."

He climbed up in to the wagon and picked up the reins; as he lifted the reins to start the horse, he heard his mother yell out, "Stop!"

"What is it?" he asked turning around to make sure Emma, and the baby hadn't fallen.

"I wanted to ask you to show me how to hitch up the

wagon. Not today. Sometime. I can visit Emma and baby Timmy. And your new baby too."

"Sure, Mama."

"Thank you."

John lifted reins and slapped them down. His horse took off with a jolt, Emma held on to the sides to keep from falling off the bench. Timmy fell back in his carrier and just laughed.

Claire watched until they were out of sight. She had just enough time to freshen up before Dr. Baker arrived.

Thirty minutes later, Claire finished washing up, she removed the from her hair and rewound the bun before securing again at the top of her head. As she walked out of her bedroom, she heard his buggy pull up.

She grabbed her shawl and hat. Claire put her hat on and tied the bow under her chin. She carried her shawl; the air was warm from the April sun but once the sunset, it would be much cooler. She didn't know how long she would be gone. Claire heard a buggy and quickly, step outside to greet the doctor.

Dr. Baker stepped down from his horse-drawn carriage. She was thankful it had a roof covering since there wasn't a cloud in the sky.

"Claire, before we take off, I want to talk to you."

"About Lukas?"

"About Lukas," he replied. "When I examined Lukas in the barn, he was in a vegetated state. He couldn't move his legs, his arms, he couldn't talk. He barely squeezed my hand. To be honest, I'm not sure he did."

They walked to the bench and sat down.

"Go on," Claire said apprehensively.

"This morning, I walked into the ward and Lukas was sitting up. Complaining about being there. Like yesterday didn't happen."

"That man. He's a grouser. Always been stubborn as a mule. He refused to stay in bed when he was sick. Never missed a day of work. Insisted on milking cows when he was sick as a dog."

"Yes, he is a stubborn man."

"But, Dr., what is wrong with Lukas?"

"I'm getting there," Dr. Baker said. "First, I thought he suffered palsy or a stroke. But his overnight recovery doesn't match up with the usual symptoms. There are no lingering issues."

"You said he recovered? Talking, walking, everything?" Claire interrupted.

"Yes, he can talk, walk. Yes. Everything is normal."

"But something was wrong with him yesterday."

"Yes, I know. I saw him. There was something wrong with him. But I was at a loss to find the cause. I couldn't find anything in my medical books. It was a mystery."

With her finger pressed against her pursed lips, Claire pondered his comments. Nothing wrong with him. Her forehead wrinkled as she thought about it.

"Can I ask you a few questions about his mood lately?"

"Lukas has been down in dumps. But it's been worse since the trial and the not guilty verdict. He doesn't talk to anyone. Or at least, not me.'

"Anything else?"

"It goes further back–back to when we lost Gracie and Timmy. Although, I don't think he grieved for Gracie. Just Timmy. He was kind and supportive during the funeral. That all ended after the funeral. We came home after the service at the cemetery. We all knew it would be hard, but we had each other. Or I thought we did. Lukas changed his clothes and left without saying a word. He stopped going to church, but you probably knew that."

Dr. Baker nodded. Before the murders, the Johansson family arrived early for the service and proudly sat in the front pew; now Claire sat alone in the back of the church.

"Since then, he's barely spoken to me. He grunts or mumbles something I can't hear and will only say something if he has no other choice. Now that the children have all moved out, there is a deafening silence. He sits at the table waiting for his supper but doesn't ask. He finishes his meal and walks away. After eating, he retires for the night. He rises early before me and leaves without a meal. Sometimes, he is gone for hours.

He goes to the cemetery several times a week. I know cuz the caretaker told us. Sometimes, he sits at the stone and talks; other times he lies on ground and cries."

"Does he say anything to you?"

"He blames me for Timmy's death. No, he hasn't talked to me;

not like we did before all this. He bl.. blames me for Timmy." Claire's voice cracked. Tears escaped her eyes. She quickly wiped them away with her hand.

Dr. Baker couldn't believe what he heard.

The weeks following the death of their children, Claire attributed her husband's silence to his grief. Until she confronted him. Claire remembered that day like it was yesterday. Excitement filled the room. Anna Belle's recent engagement to Robert and John and Emma's baby announcement; she couldn't be happier. The family needed these diversions. Everyone, full of excitement, laughed and hugged and talked at once until Lukas walked into the parlor. They felt his presence like a dark cloud around them. He came in to see what caused the ruckus. He didn't smile or seem excited after hearing the news. Disappointed with his reaction, Claire assured her children "he would come around."

After a short visit, John and Emma left for home. Anna Belle and Chloe sat with their noses in the Sears & Roebuck catalog giggling with excitement. Claire quietly left the room and found Lukas lying in bed. The quilt pulled up to his chin. His eyes were closed, but she knew he wasn't asleep. She wasted no time with any small talk. She asked why he didn't talk to her. And that's when he said, "You killed my boy. It's all your fault my son is dead. You forced him to go to church that night. And now he is gone forever."

Claire's eye welted as she whispered, "He blames me for Timmy's death. Because I encouraged them to go to church Sunday night. How could I know what would have happened? They had gone to church a hundred times with no harm." Claire paused, "What does this have to do with yesterday?"

"Yesterday was the anniversary of their deaths. The caretaker said Lukas was at the cemetery yelling out crazy things. He said he had seen him there many times but this time it was different. Lukas said he would Timmy soon."

"I know, the caretaker has told both John and me about his visits."

"The caretaker saw something different this time. He feared Lukas might do something drastic. When we rolled Lukas over, his shotgun was underneath him."

"Oh, he must have found a critter in the barn. I'm sure that was it. Take his own life? He wouldn't do that. What are you saying, Dr. Baker? No, no, no! He would never do that. He wouldn't," Claire said firmly. Or would he?

"Claire, hear me out. He could not talk. He could not move his legs. His hands. He stared blankly at nothing. He didn't see me. Or you. Or the detectives. Like he was in a trance. And today, he is talking and walking and aware of where he is. I could find nothing to explain what ailed him."

"So, what are you saying, Dr. Baker?"

"I believe Lukas is suffering from Melancholia."

"Mel-melan. Colia, cholia? What's that?" Claire never heard of it or anyone suffering it.

"Depression. Severe depressed state."

"Lukas! Insane. You are saying he's insane," Claire shook her head in disbelief.

"Not insane. Depressed. Just depressed. He had all the symptoms. Abnormal motor skills, unable to speak, walk. In a vegetative state. Trance-like. Overnight recovery."

"Is there a cure?"

"Not really. It could happen again."

"It could. How will I know when?"

"We don't know how or when they will occur."

"He hasn't smiled since the children died. He keeps to himself. It has gotten worse since the not guilty verdict. Oh, what about the news about Jacob?"

"He could have another bout. Or never again. Right away or months from now. Another trial could set it off. Or another anniversary. Or just a brief memory. Claire, I'm sorry to burden you with this. You need to watch for signs."

"Will he have to go live in the asylum?" Claire had heard rumors of the conditions and treatments at the asylum. Patients locked in rooms screaming and shrieking all day long, unsanitary conditions with dirty bedsheets, slop for food inedible to animals. Lukas wouldn't last a day.

"No. No, they institutionalize only the severe cases."

"What will you tell Lukas?"

"Nothing. I will tell him I can't find anything wrong with him." How do you tell someone they are suffering from severe depression?

"I don't think he will care. He wants to go home. Get out of there."

"It will satisfy Lukas with hearing there isn't any medically wrong with him. He'll complain that I wasted his time."

Yes. He will complain," Claire agreed. "He will be ha… content to go home." Claire corrected herself. She didn't think he would ever be happy again.

"I would just tell him he can go home. If he asks, I will tell him he is a medical miracle."

"That will satisfy him."

"Let's go get your husband out of the hospital."

With the help of Dr. Baker, Claire climbed up and took her seat on the bench. The doctor took his seat and grabbed the reins. Within seconds, they were on their way.

* * * * * * * * *

After her afternoon class and lecture, Lillian walked back to the nurses' living quarters. It was such a beautiful day; she thought she would take a walk around the hospital grounds before her shift started. The news of her brother's arrest and father's diagnosis weighed heavy on her mind. She ran up the steps to her room, dropped her books off and ran back outside.

"Aren't you a sight for sore eyes?"

Lillian turned around. "Benjamin!"

"Where are you going?"

"Nowhere. Just a walk before my shift starts. Need to clear my head."

"Why? Is something troubling you? Mind if I join you?" He

asked apprehensively as he looked towards the main hospital unsure of who might lurk at one of the many windows.

"Yes, please, walk with me."

They walked in silence for a few minutes. Lillian wondered where to begin and tell Benjamin what troubled her. How do you tell your future husband they arrested your brother for killing your younger brother and sister? Especially after he diagnosed Papa with depression. Lillian shook her head.

"Lil, please! Tell me what is troubling you. You worry me."

"Um, I am not sure where to start."

"Is it us? Have you changed your mind?"

"No, no, not at all," Lillian reassured him. "I still want to marry you when we are both finished our schooling."

"Thank the Lord. I was afraid that you grew weary of me. I have been researching towns nearby, the ones without doctors. I cannot wait until I marry you and working side by side every day."

"Me too. I hope you still want to after what I have to tell you."

Benjamin stopped walking. He grabbed Lillian's forearm and stopped her. She turned to look at him. Her eyes troubled.

"Tell me," he demanded. He didn't care who saw them now.

"Ah, um, my brother. Jacob. He was, uh, arrested for the murder of my sister and brother. Gracie and Timmy."

Lillian closed her eyes and wished the ground would swallow her up. She feared his reaction.

"My beautiful Lily open your eyes," he said.

She slowly opened her eyes. Benjamin stood in front of her. He didn't look scared or ready to run. His eyes full of love for her.

"Lily, I will never leave you. Not for this. Not for anything"

"But, my papa."

"No, not because of your papa, your brother or anyone else. It is you I want to marry. Get that silly idea out of your head."

At that moment, Lillian wanted to hug Benjamin, but she knew, she couldn't. They stood in the gardens outside the hospital; someone could see them. Although, their mutual adoration for each other was obvious to everyone at the hospital, it was best not to flaunt it. The head nurse and doctors turned a blind eye toward their courtship, but still, relationships frowned upon. From the day they met, it was love at first sight. A stolen glance as they cross paths, a flirty smile when discussing a patient or a quick wink when their paths crossed in the hallway. So instead, she smiled.

CHAPTER 14

Jacob put down his spoon, wiped his mouth with his napkin and said, "That was great, Chloe!"

"Yes, it was!" Charles agreed. Chloe's husband stood up and motioned for Jacob to follow him into the parlor. Jacob obliged as Chloe cleaned up the dishes.

In the other room, Charles picked up his pipe laying on the mantle. With his other hand, he ran a match down the front of the fireplace and held the lit end to the pipe as he inhaled. As he exhaled, the aroma of the tobacco filled the air.

He turned towards Jacob who now sat on the couch. "What are your plans?"

"I'm not sure of your question. I am meeting with my attorney tomorrow. I need to work on my farm without run-ins with Papa," Jacob responded thinking the question was odd.

"How long do you plan on staying here?"

"I haven't thought that far ahead. I would prefer to stay at my home but with Papa so close, I am not sure if that is possible." Jacob thought for a second. It appeared Charles didn't want him there. He added, "I don't want to be a burden. I can stay at my farm." Jacob stood halfway.

"Charles Carter!" Chloe yelled out from the kitchen door. "Jacob, sit down. There will be no talk of Jacob leaving. Not right now."

A dumbfound Charles looked at his wife in disbelief. But not wanting to appear weak in front of his brother-in-law, Charles rebuked, "I made no mention of Jacob leaving today. I merely wanted to know his plans."

"His plans are to fight and…"

"I can speak for myself, Chloe!" Jacob interrupted. "I will fight this. I am not guilty." I think. Jacob still couldn't remember what happened that night.

Just blocks away, Dr. Baker halted the buggy in front of the Johansson farm. Next to him, Lukas sat. He hadn't spoken the entire ride. That was unusual since Lukas didn't use to be at a loss for words, especially when he disagreed with something. Lukas accepted the unknown diagnosis. And rejoiced in being called a medical miracle.

"I told you nuthin' vuz vong vith me," he mumbled as he left the hospital.

"Thank you, Dr. Baker, for bringing us home," Claire said from the back of the buggy. "Come on, Lukas, we need to let the good doctor go home to his family."

"Oh, ja," Lukas said as he jumped out of the buggy and walked away without a word.

Claire eyed him and said, "Please, Dr. Baker, excuse his rudeness."

"No problem, Claire, no problem," he replied. Dr. Baker had been the family doctor and friend of the family for many years. He accepted Lukas for who he was, then continued with, "I will check tomorrow to see how he is doing."

"Thank you, again, Doctor."

Dr. Baker lifted his reins, and, with a snap, the horse moved. Claire stood and watched him disappear down the road.

Inside, Claire found Lukas at the basin washing his face. "Do you want me to make you supper now?" She knew he hadn't eaten since breakfast.

"Nah." Lukas picked up his hat and placed it on his head.

"Where are you going?"

"Barn," he grumbled.

"Daniel has taken on more chores. He plowed the fields. He said they are ready to plant."

"Can't plant now."

"After the last frost," Claire said. She grew up on this farm and well knew of the planting seasons.

Lukas walked out the door and headed down the path towards the barn. Inside the barn, Daniel sat in front of the furthest cow, his hands worked the udders and filled the pail. When it was full, he stood up to carry to the tin cans.

"Hey, old man! Feeling better?" Daniel dumped the contents of the pail. A few cats lingered and lapped up the milk drops.

"Nutting vuz vong vith me."

"If you say so. I finished plowing the fields," Daniel said as he picked up the stool and sat down in front of the next cow.

"Good," Lukas mumbled.

"I got everything under control here. You go rest or something."

"I don't need no rest. I rested all day. Vasted a full day doing nothing. Nothing is vong with me. I told him that."

"Suit yourself," Daniel said as he placed the stool by the second cow.

Lukas leaned up against the wall; his arms folded across his chest. He thought about pulling up a stool and helping with the milking but with only had six cows, Daniel would finish in no time.

"Shocking news about Jacob," Daniel said as he stood up to carry another full pail to the milk cans.

"Uh, vat?"

"Jacob, the news."

"What news about Jacob?"

"His arrest."

"His arrest? For what? Drunkenness?"

"For the murders."

"The murders?"

"Yea, Timmy and Gracie."

Lukas straightened up. He dropped his arms and clenched his fists. His mouth hung open. He couldn't believe what he had just heard.

"Jacob murdered my son!" Lukas yelled out. "Jacob did it!"

I should have kept my mouth shut, Daniel thought.

"Jacob killed my boy!" Lukas yelled out again as he stormed out of the barn. He shut the door so hard, the wall shook.

He continued to yell out as he stomped towards the house. He yelled as he briskly walked towards the house; "He dodade min boy. I am going to doda honom. Jag kommer att döda honom with my bare hands. Han tog min son away from me. Han är inte bra och förtjänar inte att leva[1]," He repeated the last sentence in English, "He's no good and doesn't deserve to live."

Claire stood over the stove and stirred the contents of the soup pot. She stared down and watched the broth bubble as the stew heated. She heard Lukas' rants in a mixture of English and Swedish as he got closer to the house. *What is he is angry about now?* The back door flung open and slammed closed with a such force the walls shook.

---

[1]He killed my boy. I am going to kill him. I will kill him with my bare hands. He took my son away from me. He is not good and does not deserve to live," He repeated the last sentence in English, "He's no good and doesn't deserve to live."

"Jacob murdered my boy! Why haven't I been told this? Vat are you not telling me?"

Claire froze. The spoon fell from her hand and dropped against the side of the pot with a bang. She looked up at Lukas. His eyes filled with anger.

"Lukas! Now calm down. Please. I planned to tell you after supper. You were in the hospital. Do you remember seeing Chief Morrow and Detective Maloney yesterday in the barn? They stop here to tell you and that is when they found you laying on the ground. Please, Lukas. Please sit down," Claire pleaded as Lukas paced the floor.

"He killed my son. He killed Timmy, my boy, my precious boy."

Lukas stomped into the bedroom and came out with this shotgun.

"Lukas, wait! Where are you going?"

"To find that no good murderer."

"Lukas! I beg of you to put your gun down. Sit. Let's talk first."

"No. I have to go find Jacob."

"You won't find him at home."

"Is he in jail?"

Claire bit her lip and said, "Yes, he is in jail." Lord, forgive me for lying! For Jacob's sake, she needed to hide the truth.

Lukas lowered his shotgun to his side. "He deserves to be locked up. I hope he rots in jail. Or they hang him. I forbid you to help him. Do you hear me?"

"Lukas, please. Settle down."

"I said you will not help him. Do ya hear me?"

"Yes, Lukas. I hear you."

Claire picked up the ladle and filled a bowl with the soup. She placed it on the table where Lukas usually sat. She pushed the basket of breads in front of the bowl. She then placed a cup on the table by his bowl and retrieved the coffeepot from the stove. She poured the piping hot coffee and turned to put the pot back to stove.

Lukas stood and watched Claire set the table with his supper. Without a second thought, he leaned his shotgun against the wall in the corner. He grudgingly walked to his chair and sat down. He picked up his spoon and dug in; never saying a word.

With her back towards Lukas, Claire smiled. Even as mad as he was, she knew he had eaten little in the past few days. She turned slightly to watch him lift a heaping spoonful in to his mouth. Within a few minutes, he dropped his spoon into the empty bowl and pushed it away from him. He stood and retreated to their bedroom. His shotgun left in the corner.

* * * * * * * * *

The next morning, Jacob woke up to the sound of voices coming from the kitchen. With his door closed, he couldn't make out any words, but he could tell it was a heated discussion between his sister and her husband.

Jacob crawled out of bed. Wearing just his breeches, he walked around the bed to the dresser. He picked up the pitcher and poured water into the basin. He lowered his cupped hands into the water and splashed his face. He then ran his wet hands through his hair and dried in face and hands on the embroidered hand towel hanging over the bar.

He needed to use the privy but the conversation in the other room continued and he didn't want to interrupt them. He didn't want to be the reason for any discord between them. Today, he would find another place to stay. He slipped into his trousers, tucked in his shirt, and buttoned the suspenders.

He heard a door slam close and guessed that Charles had left for work. Not wanting to cause his sister any more hardship, he quickly made the bed before he opened the bedroom door. He listened for a second to make Charles had left and upon hearing no more conversation; he closed the bedroom and walked towards the kitchen.

In the kitchen, he found Chloe standing in front of the stove. He watched as she flipped the eggs over.

"Morning'," Jacob announced.

Chloe turned to face Jacob and with a smile, said, "Good morning, Jacob. I hope you found the bed comfortable."

"Yea, I did." Jacob looked around and asked, "Charles already gone?"

"Yes, he left a few minutes ago. Please, sit down and have breakfast. Fried eggs?"

"Sounds good." Jacob wasn't much of a cook. He appreciated

his mother's generosity and had mastered the art of reheating food. Occasionally, he accepted her invitation to eat breakfast with her and she treated him to a hearty meal with all the works; eggs, ham, biscuits, and gravy.

Chloe placed the fried eggs on the plate and carried to the table. She poured him a cup of coffee and said, "There is a few biscuits left too."

Jacob sat down in front of the plate with the two sunny side up eggs and a slab of fried ham. With his fork, he poked the yolks. He watched as the thick yellow yolk ran out covering the whites of the egg. He scooped up some eggs with his fork and continued eating until his plate was empty. He split a biscuit in half and ran it across his plate clearing away every bit of the yolk.

When he had completely cleared his plate, he placed his fork down and picked up his coffee.

"Thank you, Chloe. Yum. Your biscuits taste like Mama's."

"Of course, they do, silly, I learned from Mama. What are you doing today?"

"I am meeting with my attorney this morning. Then I will head up to John's farm to plan how I will work on my farm and live next to Papa."

Later that morning, Jacob stepped out of the brick building. He felt his meeting with the attorney went well. In about three weeks, the grand jury would meet, and decide if the evidence calls for a trial.

Jacob perked up when he heard the news, but Attorney Hammill shot him down at once. "I don't believe the grand jury will go against the police department."

His attorney felt he could win this one. He had already worked on his defense strategy.

Jacob walked towards the trolley station and thought about what Hammill told him. The trial won't be until late Fall. Seven months away! How was he going to survive seven more months?

But that wasn't the only thing troubling Jacob? Jacob just didn't understand why.

Jacob hopped on the trolley. Instead of taking a seat, he stepped aside so a middle-aged lady could sit. She smiled as she passed him. Jacob liked that he was a nobody. Just another rider. Not the brother of two murder siblings or the arrested suspect in the murders. He was just a regular person riding the trolley out of downtown.

The trolley reached the station and Jacob jumped off; he headed up Sixth Ave towards John's farm. He wished he had his wagon but didn't want to take a chance of running into his father.

As he walked passed Water's Restaurant, he remembered that Gracie and Timmy had stopped that night for candy. The candy that scattered all over the gravel road. Jacob never visited the murder site; other than he walked by when running errands. He didn't stop. After the funeral, he walked passed it but by the then, someone had taken away everything.

Two women came out of the dry goods store and almost ran into Jacob. They recognized Jacob right away. One turned to the other and whispered. Across the street, two old men sat in front of a barber shop playing checkers. They didn't hide their curiosity. Jacob just looked straight ahead and continued walking. If only he could disappear until after the trial.

Thirty minutes later, Jacob arrived at John's farm. He walked up to the front door, raised his arm to knock when he heard his name called out.

He turned to see John in the field across the way. Jacob turned and walked in his direction.

"Did you meet with the attorney today?"

"Yeah," Jacob said. "Grand jury hearing in three weeks. Trial late Fall."

"That is a long wait. I talked to Emma's brothers, Jimmy, and Davey. We got it figured out."

"Huh?"

"Your farm."

"Oh, yeah."

"We will take turns working your farm. You will stay here with us and work the farms up here. Jimmy and Davey work the family farm and Davey has a few acres up the road."

"Gee, thanks. I have the creamery job. Or I think I do. I haven't talked to him."

"We'll go into town. We can stop there. Then get your things from the house."

"I don't know about that."

"And your wagon. We will make sure Papa isn't around. We even cut around the back way so not to pass the farm. How ready are you to plant?"

"I plowed my fields and ready for seed. I never picked up the seed."

"We will stop there. I have to pick up mine too."

John sense Jacob's apprehension and asked, "What's the problem?"

"The whispering and gossiping in town. Downtown nobody knew who I was but in Highland Park, they all do."

"I will sit next to you," John said as he slapped his hand on Jacob's shoulder. "Let's take this old girl to the barn and see what Emma's made for supper."

With the mule settled in her stall, the two brothers made their way into the house. Inside, the kitchen table already set with two bowls full of piping hot stew. A fresh loaf of bread between them. Emma nowhere in sight.

As they sat down and ate, Emma returned from the bedroom.

"Timmy was tuckered out. He fell asleep sitting in his chair," she chuckled. "Is the stew still hot?"

"Yes, Emma, it is," Jacob said.

"Jacob and I are going into town, pick up supplies and his wagon. Jimmy and Davey are coming later tonight to discuss our plans for Jacob's farm."

"I have Jacob's room ready for him. I hope you can handle our rambunctious boy. And this one too when it finally arrives." Emma placed a hand on her belly.

"No problem. I appreciate everything you are doing to help me. I know I haven't been the best brother," Jacob said then looking at Emma added. "Or brother-in-law, lately."

"Water under the bridge, Jacob, water under the bridge," Emma added.

My family is supporting me. Even though I have been a grouser all my life. Jacob vowed that when all of this was behind them, he would be a better person.

John and Jacob stopped at the farm supply store. The farmers leaving the building stopped and stared when they recognized Jacob.

"Do you want to stay here or come in with me?" John asked.

Jacob looked around. He didn't think it mattered whether the people stared at him outside on the street or inside the shop.

"I'll go in with you."

They walked into the store. In the store's back, the owner chatted with a few farmers. Jacob recognized the men—both regular stops on his creamery run. As they walked to the back, the conversation stopped. The three men looked at Jacob.

"Good afternoon," Jacob addressed the farmers.

The farmers nodded, picked up their purchases and walked out of the store.

"Can I help you?"

"We are here to pick up our seed orders. Johansson. Jacob and John."

"Got them in back," the store owner said as he walked away. He returned a few minutes later with a burlap bag over his shoulder. He swung onto the counter and disappeared again. He threw the second bag on the counter in front of Jacob.

"I believe that's all you ordered."

"Yes, that's it," John said as he pulled money out of his coat pocket. Jacob realized he had no money with him. "You can pay me back."

The brothers threw the burlap bags over their shoulders and walked out to the wagon. After they stowed the bags in the back, they left.

"Creamery?"

"Yes. After that, can we run by Isabelle's?"

"Yeah."

Jacob met with the creamery owner. Because of the publicity, the owner decided that Jacob shouldn't work for him anymore. At least, not until after the trial. Dejected, Jacob climbed back into the wagon.

"I won't be working there for a while."

"Sorry. I know you needed the extra money."

"Yeah."

John snapped the reins, and the wagon moved. Jacob gave John directions to Isabelle's family home. When they pulled up, Jacob jumped out of the wagon and walked towards the house. Isabelle met him halfway. Jacob could tell by the look in her eyes, she knew.

"Jacob, I heard the news."

"Yeah, I wanted to stop by to tell you I will stay up North by the coal mines for a few months. At my brother's. Until after the trial."

"Jacob, my papa said you can't come calling anymore. I can't be seen with you."

Jacob looked down. He had expected this.

"Yeah. That's what I expected," he said as he turned away.

"Jacob, I'm sorry."

Jacob kept on walking. He climbed into the wagon and said, "Let's go!"

They road in silence. John wondered how to comfort his brother. First, his job and now, his girl. What do you say to someone who's life is turned upside down? He knew whatever he said wouldn't change a thing.

Jacob wondered if his life would ever be the same again. He lost a job he held for four years and the girl he thought he would marry. And to top it off, a murder trial loomed over his head. Forced to farm another man's land and move out of his house; afraid to cross paths with his father for fear of how he could react. His life was a mess.

They took the long way to Jacob's. When they arrived, John pulled behind the house. Jacob ran inside using the back door. A few minutes later, he came out with his sack packed full. He ran to the barn, came out with a horse, and hitched the horse to his wagon. Meanwhile, John unloaded one of the seed bags and carried in to the barn.

"We had better git out of here."

"Yea," Jacob replied as he climbed into the wagon. He snapped the reins and headed north on Poor Farm Road. He turned back to look at his house one last time. He didn't know when or if would ever come back.

John followed Jacob. He knew it troubled his brother. He lost so much these past few days.

* * * * * * * * *

Lillian carried the empty trays to the table by the door. With only five patients in the ward, she would have time to catch up on her studies.

She carefully stacked the empty cups, plates, and utensils on the trays. The on-duty nurse took them to the kitchen after the patients were down for the night. She turned to check the ward. Two of the men read the newspaper while another wrote a letter. The other men rested. She slipped out quietly to take the trays to the kitchen.

As she walked down the hallway, her mind wondered about her family. She didn't talk to or even see her mother today. Not after hearing the news about Jacob.

Halfway down the hallway, Lillian froze. The trays slipped out of her hands and fell to the floor.

Cling, clang! The metal plates banged against each other and the sound echoed down the empty hallway.

He said I'm sorry. At the funeral home. He said I'm sorry to Gracie.

"What's all the commotion?"

She looked up to see her friend, Susannah, coming out of another ward to investigate the loud noise.

Lillian's face lacked color. Her mouth hung open. She didn't bend down to pick up the trays.

"Lillian, are you feeling ill? You look like you saw a ghost."

Lillian turned to her friend and said, "He said I'm sorry. He said I'm sorry to Gracie."

"What? Who?"

"Jacob. At the funeral home. When we went to say our final goodbyes. He bent down and whispered to Gracie, I'm sorry. I thought it was strange. Why would he apologize? And now they arrested him. Was he apologizing because he did it?"

"Oh, no, Lillian. That can't be true. Maybe, you misunderstood him."

Susannah bent down and stacked up the trays and metal plates. Lillian joined her as she scooped up the forks and spoons that had scattered all over the hallway.

Susannah went back into her ward and returned with a wet rag. She wiped the floor and stood up. Lillian still knelt in front of her. Susannah reached down and grabbed her hands to pull up. She then bent down and picked the stacked trays.

"I will run these to the kitchen for you. Go back to the ward and try to forget this. We have an exam tomorrow morning."

"I don't know if I can."

"Lillian, there is nothing you can do about this right now. After our class, we will figure this out."

"Oh, I need to study."

Lillian watched Susannah walked away. She turned and slowly walked back to her ward. Loud snores filled the room. The two men slept unaware they sounded like a train barreling by. She walked across the room and pulled their curtains close so not to disturb the others.

She stopped at the foot of the bed of one man. "How are you feeling tonight?"

"Doc says my fever broke. I can go home soon."

"That's good news. I will miss you. You still need your rest. Just a few more minutes of reading before I have to turn the lights off."

Lillian turned to the other two beds to see if they had heard her.

"I need to finish this letter to my daughter. Would you mind helping me? I am having trouble with my spelling."

"Of course, I will help you," Lillian said as she pulled a chair next to his bed. He handed her the pencil and paper. "Now, what else do you want to say?"

For twenty minutes, Lillian listened as Mr. Oxford told her what to say; sometimes straying from their task to tell her a funny antidote or story. When they had finished, she wrote the address on an envelope and placed in her pocket.

"I will post this tomorrow for you."

"Thank you, you are kind, Miss Lillian."

Lillian smiled and announced, "Light's out. You all need to rest so you can go home to your families."

Lillian walked across the room and turned the lights off. The patients laid down and within minutes; they were asleep. Loud breathing and snores filled the room.

Lillian sat down at the nurses' table. The lamp on the table the only illumination. She opened her book and read. She found her mind wandering back to the awful day last year when they buried Gracie and Timmy.

No, I can't think about this right now. I need to study. Tomorrow, I will go to the police station and tell them about Jacob.

Two hours later, Lillian felt chilled. She looked to see the fire dwindling down. She quickly threw in two logs and some kindling; the fire grew and warmed the room.

I better get more logs and kindling, or the fire will go out.

"Psst," she heard from the door.

Susannah stood in the opening, she whispered loudly, "I'm going down to get firewood."

"I will go with you," Lillian said as she looked back at the men all sound asleep.

The two students walked down the hall to the large staircase.

"It will be nice when the nights are warm, and we don't have to tend to the fire too."

"I almost let the fire go out," Lillian admitted. "I was studying and forgot it."

The two ran down the steps and around to the back of the building. Outside the kitchen door, they loaded their arms with firewood and kindling and made their way back upstairs.

"Just a few more months and we won't have to work overnight," Susannah sighed.

* * * * * * * * *

Claire heard Lukas in the kitchen washing up. She opened her eyes and discovered the sun hadn't risen yet. Why is up so early?

Claire climbed out of bed, grabbed her night coat, and left the room. She slipped her hands into the sleeves as she walked into the kitchen.

"You are up early. I will make coffee." Clare tied the ribbon on her coat as she walked to the stove.

"No time. Need to finish plowing," he grumbled back. "Too much rain last year. Fields are muddy."

Claire understood. Last summer, it rained every other day. The pond behind the farm well over its banks. The Farmer's Almanac predicted another wet spring. She prayed it wasn't correct.

CHAPTER 15

A few miles north, John and Emma's brothers left early to work at Jacob's farm. The night before the three men along with Jacob devised a plan that would work for all of them. Jacob envied his brother marrying into such a generous family.

Meanwhile, Jacob walked over to their family's farm work with Emma's father, Mr. Tucker. Jacob felt apprehensive to work with Mr. Tucker due to his own relationship with his father. Mr. Tucker was easy going and nothing like Lukas. He didn't criticize for not knowing how to do something. He took a few extra minutes to show him. He didn't complain about Jacob's problems interfering with his own family. For most of the morning, Jacob and Mr. Tucker repaired the fences. Mr. Tucker asked questions as they worked.

"How many acres do ya got?" Mr. Tucker sat down on a tree stump.

"Just twenty-six. I hope to buy more someday." Jacob climbed over the fence to retrieve a fallen fence post.

"Ya' bought that farm all by yourself?"

"Yep. Saved my money for years. Got it a few days after my eighteenth birthday."

"You're hardworking young man. Buying a farm at your age. Me. This was pappy's land then my papa's and now mine."

He talked about how his father's family came to be in Iowa. How his grand pappy squatted the very land they worked on in the mid-1830's. His father the first in his family born on Iowa soil.

Jacob asked lots of questions. His own grandfather died long before Jacob could ask questions. His father didn't waste time on idle chitchat. In fact, none of his siblings knew about his family back in Sweden.

"Well done, son," he heard Mr. Tucker say when they hammered the last post. Jacob nodded and hid his smile. He can't remember the last time someone complimented him. He couldn't help wishing he had been born in this family.

"Thank you, Mr. Tucker."

"George. Call me George."

Their plan worked perfectly. Jacob looked forward to working each day. The men worked hard. In two weeks, the planting completed. They celebrated with a Sunday afternoon picnic. They laughed and ate and talked the day away. No one mentioned running into Lukas; even though Jacob thought John visited their mama, the days he worked his farm. No criticism or harsh words. The Tuckers were good people.

As the sun settled in the west, Emma and her mother cleared the table leaving the men alone. George Tucker reached into his pocket and pulled out a bottle of whiskey. In his other pocket, he took out five cigars.

Mr. Tucker poured the whiskey into their cups and handed out the cigars.

"Here's to the hard work and dedication!" he said lifting his cup.

"Yeah, hard work."

Jacob hesitated as he raised his cup. It had been months since he had a drink. Or a cigar, he thought as Davey handed him the matches.

Davey and Jimmy drained their cups then them placed down in front their father. Jacob sipped his. Tomorrow was the grand jury hearing. He didn't need to feel or look sick.

The next morning, Jacob and John traveled to the hearing. Jacob sat with Robert Hammil with John seated behind him. As predicted, the judge determined there was enough evidence for a trial. A date set for November.

After the hearing, they met with the attorney at his office. Mr. Hammill told them his defense plans for the trial. He talked about a string of murders in Denver. He told them about the evidence provided by the District Attorney's office. Both brothers stunned by the evidence.

"How can that be?" John questioned. Jacob too stunned to even talk.

"Let me worry about this. The District Attorney will not want to lose a second trial, so I am expecting a fight. But I have my own tricks up my sleeve. And I will fight back."

Jacob and John rose to leave. They shook the attorney's hand and walked out.

"Are you as stunned as I am?" John asked.

"More," Jacob said. "How could she?"

"Anna Belle had her baby. Want to stop in?"

"Yeah."

They stopped at the livery to pick up their wagon. The large negro greeted at the door.

"Where's Jerry?" Jacob asked.

"Jerry had a meeting. Representing Highland Park. Something 'bout the river north. I'm Willie. Willie Hobbs." He held out his hand.

"Nice to meet you," John said.

"Me and my mama are running' the place now. Missus Martin taught me arithmetic. I know how to add and subtract."

"Good for you."

"Ya back for your wagon?"

"Yea."

"I ga' him all brushed down for ya. He's a fine horse."

"Thank ya. How much do I owe?"

"Twenty-five cents."

John pulled out a quarter and handed it to him. Willie pointed to his horse and wagon by the door.

"Yup. He's a fine horse."

John grabbed the bridle and led the horse and wagon out the stable doors. Willie followed them and said, "You have a good day!"

"Good day!" John yelled back.

As soon as they left, Willie went straight for the office. He sat at the desk and opened the ledger book. In neat penmanship, he wrote "25 cents". He looked down at the ledger and said, "Mizz Martin would give me "A" for that."

"What did you say?"

"Oh, mama. Just admiring my penmanship. Looky here. Look at the curves of the two and five. Mizz Martin would tell me they were fine looking numbers."

"You better watch yourself, boy, or you will get a big head."

She turned to walk out of the office, but quickly turned around, "I almost forgot why I was here. I got dinner on the stove if you are hungry. Mutton stew."

"Hmm-hmmm! Always hungry for your cooking,' mama."

Rosie Hobson smiled with her back turned from her son. She was proud of him. Although limited, her son could read and write; something a child of a slave never learns to do.

The excitement in Willie's eye when he told her of Jerry Martin's offer forever embedded in her mind. He burst into the house talking so fast she couldn't understand a word he said. He called for his father to join them from behind the blanket wall. His father slowly hobbled in to the main area; sat down at the rustic table in the sparsely furnished room. His mama told him to slow down and tell them what excited him.

At first, Rosie didn't believe her ears. Jerry Martin offered her son an opportunity to run the livery as he pursued a political career. His wife, a former teacher, would tutor Willie in the skills necessary to run the daily operations of the livery business. A chance of a lifetime!

A chance for her son to leave a life of hard labor in coal mines followed by years of ill health. Her husband and his father suffered every day; his lungs filled with the black dust as he gasped for air with every breath. Willie's lungs already affected. To Rosie that was enough to save her son.

Willie continued, "Mama, there is an apartment that all of us can live in."

"All of us? Away from the coal mines?" Jerry's offer extended to his mama and papa.

"But my job?"

"You won't have to work anymore." Rosie had worked her entire life. Born to slave parents, Rosie learned to cook at the tender age of five; working next to her mama in the plantation owner's kitchen. Sometimes, the owner's daughter would sneak into the kitchen and share her dolls. But most the time she dried dishes or washed fruits or vegetables.

When Rosie turned twelve, her mama died from dysentery and Rosie took over the kitchen duties. That same year, the owner bought a new slave–a young rugged and handsome slave named Jack. Jack worked in the stable and Rosie found excuses to take scraps for the horses.

Shortly after Rosie and Jack married, President Lincoln signed the Emancipation Proclamation, and they became paid employees. After years of miscarriages and stillborn births, Willie was born. A ten-pound baby. A strong-willed boy, hence, his name. Will. They left the plantation when he turned seven and headed for Iowa.

Rosie walked back to their apartment behind the livery. The two-bedroom apartment was huge compared to their one-room shack by the coal mines. The lower level included a full kitchen with indoor plumbing and electricity. There also was a parlor and a privy. Away from the drafty one-room cabin, Willie's father's health improved, and Rosie Hobbs felt blessed each day.

Rosie thanked God for Jerry Martin every day. "Jerry Martin is good people," she said daily. He deserved to be a city councilman. He heard the rumors of corruption in the city hall. Rosie shook her head in disgust. Prostitution at City Hall. *Tsk, tsk, tsk!* She thought. Mr. Martin will clean it up.

John steered the wagon towards their sister's house. Her baby girl arrived just a few days ago.

"Hey, did ya notice? That negro didn't know who I was. He got to be the only person in Highland Park."

"Maybe, he doesn't read the paper. Doesn't read."

"He must a good man since Jerry Martin trusts him with his business."

"You know, I think he was that coal miner they arrested first."

"You might be right."

It didn't take long to get to Anna Belle's house. Chloe greeted them at the door.

"It won't be long for you," Jacob said.

"I still have a few more months. Wait until you see her baby. Cute as a button."

"How's Anna Belle?"

"She's tired but mama's in there with her."

"Mama?" Jacob asked. He didn't think he could face her right now. The news of her involvement in his arrest still fresh in his mind. How could she think it was me?

"I'll see if Anna Belle is awake."

Chloe left the room. A few minutes, Claire came running in.

"John! Jacob! It's so good to see you!" Claire greeted her sons. John leaned down and gave his mother a peck on the cheek. She turned to Jacob, Jacob leaned in but barely grazed her skin.

"Come see your niece," she said grabbing their hands. Claire unaware of Jacob's anger towards her.

Anna Belle sat on the bed, pillows propped up against the headboard. Her pink nightgown tied in a bow at her neck. Her hair unpinned and cascaded down again her shoulders. Her baby girls swaddled and asleep on her arms. She looked tired but happy.

"Meet Elizabeth Claire!"

John and Jacob walked over to the side of the bed and looked down at their niece. With her pudgy cheeks and tiny nose, she looked like a cherub.

"Her hair is so blonde you can't see it," she laughed. Elizabeth wrinkled her face and uttered a faint sound.

"Shh, you don't want to wake her," Claire warned. "You need to rest while she is asleep."

John took the hint. "We aren't staying. Just wanted to stop in. Emma would have my hide if I didn't. If you are feeling well next Sunday, I promised her we would come visit."

"Yes, please. And Timmy too. He needs to meet his cousin."

Chloe walked out of the room with them. She sensed something was wrong.

"Is something bothering you?"

"Jacob didn't get good news today."

"Oh, Jacob, I have been praying you would."

John walked towards the door, "Let's talk outside." Chloe and Jacob followed him.

Outside, Jacob explained to Chloe what his attorney told him. When he finished, Chloe just said one word, "Mama?" Both Jacob and John nodded.

"Have you been staying here?" John asked Chloe.

"No, mama has. She came as soon as she heard Anna Belle was ready to deliver. She will stay until Anna Belle is ready to go on her own."

Jacob stepped away from the house. "Looks like rain," John said looking towards the west.

Jacob looked at the sky. "Those are thunderstorm clouds." In the distance, thunder roared. A flash of lightning spooked the horse.

"We better get home before the storm hits. Tell mama we had to go."

"I will. Be careful."

Jacob and John sprinted towards the wagon and jumped in. Not wanting to get caught in the rain, John snapped the reins and his horse raced off. The dark clouds spread, and the blue sky disappeared. They made it back just as the first drops came down. John unhitched his horse as Jacob moved the plow into the barn.

As they left the barn, the skies opened, and the rain came down in buckets. John and Jacob ran for cover. By the time they reached the house, it drenched them.

"Let me get you a blanket!" Emma said when she saw them standing in the doorway. She ran to a cupboard and pulled out two quilts. She handed them to her husband and brother-in-law.

"Quick. You need to change out of the wet clothes before you catch the chills. Bring your clothes back here and I will hang to dry in front of the stove."

John retreated to their bedroom as Jacob went to his room. After just a few weeks, he felt more at home than anywhere else. A few minutes later, both men returned carrying their wet clothing.

Emma had placed a hanging rack in front of the stove. She took their wet clothes and hung them to dry.

John walked over to the window. The rain so hard he couldn't see the barn.

"I'm afraid this might wash away the seeds we planted."

Jacob joined him at the window. They both stared out the window and hoped their arduous work wouldn't wash away.

"Remember last year, it rained all of May and June. And I had a bumper crop."

But the rain didn't stop. It rained for days. Then stopped for a few days. And then it poured again. The ground became saturated. The river and stream levels rose quickly.

* * * * * * * * *

The dark-haired man recalled a narrow escape the year before. His step-sister and her family had been visiting for the weekend.

"Did ya hear the news? Two children killed last week in Highland Park."

"It's just awful, isn't it," the old woman said.

"Why, Mama, I am glad we don't live in Des Moines anymore. Too many crimes 'round here. Burglary, robbery and now murder. Tsk, tsk, tsk." The younger woman stuffed her fork into her mouth. With her mouth full, she said, "Ames is much safer for me and my children. Right, Horace!" Rebecca asked her husband sitting next to her.

"Yea, much safer," he grunted.

The dark-haired man just listened. He didn't care to add to their conversation. It didn't matter what he said his step-sister was always right. It was best to keep his mouth shut.

"Is that blood on your shirt?" Rebecca asked. "I would never show up for meal with blood on my shirt."

Uh-uh. Thought I got it all.

"Haven't I taught you how to kill a chicken without getting blood all over ya?" the old man asked.

"After breakfast, you change your shirt and I will wash it for you," the older woman said.

"Daddy, what happened to the pump lever?"

"It broke off."

"I heard rumors that someone beat those children to death. They said it was a pipe or something. That is what the paper said."

I need to get out of here; he thought. Does she ever stop talking! For a split second, he felt sorry for Horace.

"May I be excused?" he asked of the older man and woman. "I want to check on the cows in pasture. Make sure the fence is secure."

"How rude." Rebecca snarled at him, her lips tightly closed. "Daddy, are you going to let him interrupt me like that?

"Yes, go," the old man interrupted her. The younger man stood up and walked towards the back door.

"And bring me back the stained shirt. I will wash it when Rebecca, Horace and the children leave."

"Oh, Mama, you spoil him. Now my Horace Jr. will learn to do his wash. I read that…"

Slam. He closed the back door behind him and didn't hear the rest of Rebecca's sentence.

CHAPTER 16

By the end of May, it had rained every day that month. Some days the rain measured in inches; some days it rained "cats and dogs." The ground saturated. Farm ponds flooded. Rivers spilled over their banks.

The Des Moines River flowed through town. It passed by Highland Park before turning towards Birdland Park and downtown Des Moines. At the end of May, the river gauge rose two feet in less than twelve hours. City leaders feared the worse. Police officers dispatched to notify residents and business in the impacted areas. Switchboard operators informed of the disaster plans.

At first, the residents refused to leave their homes. The river never flooded; even last summer after three solid months of rain. But the river continued to rise. The higher it rose, the harder the rapids. The water washed up everything and anything in its way; animals, equipment and even a building. The residents finally took the threat of flooded homes and businesses seriously.

The scene downtown chaotic as business along the river scrambled to pack up and move to higher ground. Neighbors helped neighbors pack up their furniture, clothing, and animals. They opened their homes, sheds, and barns to those forced to move to higher ground. Trains and trolley cars with tracks close to the river forced to stop running.

The levees pushed to their limits. The mayor called out to all able-bodied men to help strengthen the levees to protect the power stations and build barricades to keep the water away from more property.

The river continued to rise until May twenty-ninth when it stopped. But only for a few hours. Later that night, the levees broke, leaving the southern part of Des Moines underwater.

Highland Park narrowly escaped the flooding; just the western corner felt the impact. And the trolley station. Jerry Martin organized a sand bagging team to protect the businesses in Highland Park.

Jacob and John joined the business owners, farmers, and students and worked side by side as they filled bag after bag. Whiles others carried bags and stacked them five feet high and three feet deep to build a wall. After they had secured the area, they collapsed to the ground, exhausted and hungry.

Just a few blocks away, wives, mothers and daughters of the men worked in the church's basement. They set up tables and filled those stables with stews, soups, warm rolls, breads, cookies, and pies. They filled buckets with water, grabbed clean rags and lined them up in front of the church.

Jerry Martin surveyed the men sprawled out on the ground. They looked dirty and tired. He climbed into the back of the wagon and whistled to get their attention.

Whew-whew!

When they looked up, he announced, "On behalf of all the neighbors and businesses around, we thank you for your time and work. Your efforts have kept the river from flooding Highland Park. Now, the Highland Park Methodist Episcopal Church's Women's Auxiliary is serving a potluck meal right now in the church's basement. Thank you."

A roar erupted from the men. Slowly, the men rose. The bodies ached as they walked down the street.

"Should we?" Jacob asked as his stomach growled.

"I'm starving. We can grab something quick before walking home."

Jacob and John walked down the block towards the church. Outside, some younger girls stood with buckets and wet rags. Jacob walked up to first available girl.

"Why, Jacob Johansson, as I live and breathe, I didn't expect to see you tonight."

"Adelaide, how are you doing? As pretty as ever." Jacob flirted as she handed him the wet rag.

"I'm fine. How is Isabelle these days?"

"You haven't heard. I am not courting her anymore."

"Oh," Adelaide said trying to hide her delight. "I'm sorry to hear."

"No, her papa didn't want someone to see her with me. Afraid it would ruin her reputation. Would you?"

"Do you remember who my brother is?"

"Right."

"No one's knocking on my door."

"What about me? Should I knock on your door?"

"Now you are just teasing me, Jacob."

"No. I'm serious."

Adelaide smiled and said, "I would love that, Jacob," she said giving him that flirty smile that send chills up his back.

"Hurry up! We are all dirty here," someone yelled from behind him. Jacob handed the rag back to Adelaide and said, "Who's should I ask? Your mother? Michael?"

"Michael."

"I will talk to Michael. Soon. Real soon." He ran his finger across her cheek.

Adelaide smiled as she leaned into his hand.

"Hey, pretty lady. Do I get one of those smiles too? Or do just save them for murderers?"

Jacob turned around; his fists clenched. John put his arm over Jacob's shoulders and turned him around. "Remember what the attorney said. No trouble."

They filled their plates with all kinds of goodies. Roast beef, fried chicken, potatoes, and corn bread. They sat down at table and ate.

"So much for a quick bite to eat."

"Yea, I hope Emma wasn't planning on us being back for dinner," John said. Then added, "So, when did you become sweet on Adelaide?"

"I don't know. I teased her in playground at school. She didn't like bugs. Screeched at the top of her lungs when I threw a grasshopper at her. When I was sitting in jail, she brought me a breakfast that morning. She smiled. And she made me forget I was sitting in jail."

"Do you want to call on her?"

Jacob tilted his head and thought for a second before replying with "Yeah, I do. She always was Gracie's friend but now that she is older, I think I do want to court her. I will talk to her brother some time. I can't promise much. Until this trial is over. Isabelle's father said I would ruin her reputation. Adelaide said people still point and whisper. She's got nothing to lose."

"Speaking of Isabelle, look who just walked in."

Jacob looked up to see Isabelle's father and brothers head to the food line.

"They must have been working on the other side."

"Let's get out of here."

John and Jacob stood up. A girl about twelve ran over and grabbed their dirty dishes. They thanked her and walked away.

An hour later, Jacob lay in his bed staring at the ceiling. He thought about Adelaide and Isabelle. Their personalities so different. Adelaide's flirtatious smile melted every man's heart, including his. He saw it with the judge at her brother's trial. Isabelle was straitlaced and more proper, almost prudish. The more he thought about it, the more he realized Adelaide would be the right choice. He made a promise to himself to visit her brother soon.

A few days later, the water receded, and the flooded areas left covered in mud and dead fish. The residents returned to clean up the mess before moving their furniture back in. Some returned to find their homes or buildings no longer there. As they had did before the floods, groups of volunteers helped with the clean-up.

Two weeks later, Jacob went downtown for his appointment with his attorney. He could smell the lingering effects of the flooded waters.

His attorney, lucky to be on the second floor, had no damage. But the attorney had packed up and worked from home during the flood.

Jacob left his office satisfied and encouraged. He stopped at the restaurant south of the trolley station. Where Adelaide worked.

Jacob sat down at the counter. Adelaide came out of the kitchen and stopped when she saw him.

"What can I get for you today?" she asked giving him her signature smile.

Jacob said "you" then quickly added, "For starters, that pretty little smile of yours is enough to knock a fella on his britches. What do you suggest?" Jacob looked over the menu written on chalkboard attached to the wall.

"Today's special. Pork chops with all the trimmings."

"I will have the special. And a lemonade."

Adelaide disappeared into the kitchen and returned a few minutes later, with a glass of fresh-squeezed lemonade.

"I squeezed it myself. What brings you here today?"

"Hmmm. Besides you? I had an appointment with my attorney."

"I hope it went well."

"Yes, it did. I wanted to…" A female voice interrupted his sentence.

"Miss, miss? Can we have more hot tea?" A table of matronly ladies sat a few feet away; their eyes stared at Adelaide and Jacob.

"Excuse me." She wiped her hands on her apron before picking up the metal pot from a nearby stove.

Adelaide brought the women more tea and cleared away their dirty dishes. She returned a few minutes later with a plate for Jacob.

A thick cut pork chop laid on top of boiled potatoes with a slice of cornbread filled the plate. She placed it down in front of him.

Jacob cut a piece of the pork chop. "Yum," he said as he ate it and cut another piece.

"I can't take credit for the food, just lemonade. The cook made it."

Adelaide left Jacob to his meal. She cleared off the table recently vacated by the two women. She picked up the few coins they left as a tip. She expected nothing from them after she saw them glaring at her as she talked to Jacob.

Jacob finished his meal and laid his napkin on the counter. Adelaide asked him, "Will that be all? There is warm apple pie in the kitchen."

"I don't think I eat another bite. How much?"

Adelaide told him, and Jacob pulled out a change from his pocket. He handed it to Adelaide.

"Thank you for stopping in."

"Adelaide?"

"Yes."

"Were you serious the last time we talked? About us courting?"

"Why, yes, Jacob, I was."

"I will talk to your brother."

"When?"

"Soon."

"Oh, Jacob. Did you hear about my mama? That attorney my brother had, he has been courting my mama. And now they are getting married. Isn't that wonderful?"

"Is that so? Should I talk to them?"

"No, my brother. Do you know where his house is?"

"Just past the livery?"

"He works at coal mines too."

Jacob picked up his hat and bid his goodbyes. Adelaide stood at the counter and watched him walk away. She sighed. She had dreamed of this since that first grasshopper.

Jacob walked up Sixth Avenue. He passed the livery and her brother's house. He didn't stop. Not today.

About a mile up the road, Jacob saw someone walking towards him. As fate had it, it was Michael. Adelaide's brother.

When they were just a few feet apart, Michael recognized Jacob.

"Jacob!" he called out. "Haven't seen you in these parts around in ages?"

"Michael, how ya' been?"

"Good. And you?" He realized what said. "I forgot. You are going through a lot. I know how Tommy felt."

"I, uh, I, uh want to ask you something."

"What?"

"I wanted to know, um, if I, uh, can, um, call on A..Adelaide. I know my life is uncertain right now but I, um, just met with my attorney today and he, he, um, is optimistic. Before ya say no, hear me out."

"I would not say no. It hasn't been easy for Adelaide with losing her friend and almost, her brother. I don't want someone to break her heart."

"I don't intend to. She's a sweet girl."

"I want to say yes. But if you don't mind, my mama might want a say. I will speak with my mama and let you know her answer."

"I understand. I'm staying with my brother by the coal mines. Just east of Tucker farm."

"I know the place."

The men parted ways. Jacob hoped Mrs. Landers gave his blessing.

* * * * * * * * *

With Mr. Tucker feeling ill, Jacob worked alone that day. He didn't mind; although without Mr. Tucker's constant talking, it left him to his thoughts.

The more he thought about that night, the more he remembered. And that scared him. He was afraid of what he might remember.

He recalled waking up in his farmhouse shortly after David and Harry had left. He remembered the chill in air and how uncomfortable that couch was; especially with springs sticking through the fabric. He even thought he could walk home. Surely, his mama would wait for him to return.

He recollected walking towards the door and opening it. That's all he remembered. Today.

Jacob's thought about his father and his anger intensified. I hate that man. Hate him, hate him, hate him! He pounded the nail into the fence with all his force. And continued even after the nail head had disappeared into the wood.

He took a nail and pounded it into another post.

"Whoa, whoa! I think it's dead!"

Jacob stopped hammering and turned around to see Mr. Tucker.

"I think you killed it," Mr. Tucker said. "What did that post ever do to you?"

"Nuttin.' I thought you were ill." Jacob dropped the hammer into the picked up the bucket of nails and pick it up.

"I feel better now. Looks like you got the fence all fixed. Just came to tell ya, dinner is ready."

"I will wash up and be right there." Jacob turned to walk to the barn.

"And son," Mr. Tucker said. "I know this trial is troubling you. You can talk to me. I ain't going to judge ya by your past."

Jacob just nodded. He couldn't say anything with that lump in his throat. In a few short months, Mr. Tucker has been more of a father than his own father had ever been.

CHAPTER 17

Within weeks, the floods were just a memory. For the city of Des Moines, business as usual. Home rebuilt. Business reopened. Streets cleaned.

For the Johansson's, it was the summer of changes.

Claire finally convinced Lukas to install a telephone. The dark wooden box hung in the kitchen by the towel bar. The earpiece hung on its hook on one side on the other side, on the other side, the crank bar. Two silver metal domes at the top with a mouthpiece sticking out. Claire couldn't help herself. She giggled when she looked at the telephone hanging on their wall. She thought it looked like a face.

Early that morning, Claire tended to her garden when she heard the bells from inside the house. She dropped her shovel and sprinted for the door.

Inside, she picked up the earpiece and held it to her ear as she said, "Hello!"

On the other end, she heard, "Mama Claire, this is Charles. It's

Chloe. She's."

"She's what? What, Charles? What is it?" Claire's heart pounded.

"The baby. It's coming."

"I will be there soon. To help."

"Nellie is here."

Claire forgot about the midwife. Girls didn't need their mothers, sisters, or aunts to help with childbirth.

Claire hung up the phone. She washed the dirt from her hands and face before she headed to the bedroom. After just a few hours of gardening, her dress already soiled. She changed her dress, and he removed her bonnet. Underneath, the ribbon barely held her bun place. She neatened it before putting a clean one on.

After she had dressed, she grabbed her satchel and shawl. She left when she remembered the crocheted blanket she had just finished for the baby. She retrieved the blanket, wrapped in a cloth and left the house.

Claire ran to the barn. She opened the door. No Lukas. She ran to the stable with no luck. The horse and buggy were there, so she knew he hadn't gone far.

Claire scanned the farm. She could see him in the fields across the gravel road. Claire ran to tell him the news.

"Lukas, Lukas!" she yelled running towards him.

Lukas looked up and said, "Vat?" He sounded aggravated.

"Chloe! The baby. It's coming."

"Oh," he replied gruffly.

"I am going there to help. Do you want to join me?"

"There's nothing for me to do there."

"What about supper or dinner?"

"I can fix something."

"I better hurry," Claire said as she turned to leave. Still unable to walk past the murder site, Claire walked towards Poor Farm Road. She walked swiftly towards Highland Park and arrived at Chloe's house in record time.

That was hours ago. For the rest of the morning, Claire sat on the couch and watch Charles pace. In the other room, she could hear Chloe's screams and the soothing sounds of her midwife. With every cry, Charles stopped and stared at the closed door.

"How long? I mean, 'fore the baby is born?" he asked.

Claire knew she couldn't answer that.

"Oh, Charles, please sit down." Claire encouraged as she glanced at the clock on the wall. "It's past noon. Let me fix you a bite to eat."

"Mama Claire, it's been several hours. Should the baby be here by now?"

"The baby will be here when it's ready. Let's get a bite to eat."

Claire stood up and went into the kitchen. She admired their modern kitchen with its new icebox, stove and washing machine. As soon as Charles saw Anna Belle's washer, he bought one for Chloe. Claire smiled. Both her daughters married men who doted on them.

Claire rummaged through the icebox for something to eat. She found leftover fried chicken. Claire looked around the kitchen. On the large baker's rack, a white tin cannister with "BREAD" painted on the front sat. She lifted the lid and looked inside. She pulled out the cloth wrapped baked goods. She opened it; inside several slices of bread. On the shelf, a jar of apples.

Clare set the table and called to Charles. He protested at first, but finally sat down at the table and ate.

Aaarrrgghh! A cry from the other room interrupted his meal. He turned his head to listen.

Aarrrgghh! Another one.

Chloe's screams became more frequent. Claire knew it wouldn't be much longer.

Charles ate quickly and resumed his pacing in the other room. Claire ate a bit, cleaned up and joined Charles in the parlor.

Aaarrrggghhh! Aaarrrggghhh!

Her cries more intense. Charles stood and stared at the door.

Aaarrrggghhh! Aaarrrggghhh! Aaarrrgghhh!

Chloe shrieked one more time. Then silence.

Claire strained to hear any sounds from the bedroom. She

thought she heard a sobbing or laughing or both.

Wa-wa-wa! A baby cried out.

Claire bowed her head and prayed.

"Did you hear that? It's a baby's cry!"

Charles started for the door.

"Wait! Let Nellie come tell us."

Charles stopped. "Why haven't she come out? The baby? Is the baby not healthy? Oh, no, Chloe. Something is wrong with Chloe?"

His cousin's wife died in childbirth a few years ago; leaving him a widower with four young children. Charles' eyes teared as he thought of losing Chloe.

Claire could see the worry in Charles' face. She stood up and stood next to him. She wrapped her arm around Charles waist. Having given birth to seven children, she knew the baby was just the beginning. Nellie and Chloe had more work before they could see the baby.

To Charles, it seemed like hours since he heard the baby's cry but, just twenty minutes later, the door opened, and Nellie appeared.

"You have a healthy baby boy!"

"A boy! Did you hear that I have a son?" Charles said looking at his mother-in-law.

"How wonderful! Another boy!" Claire responded. "I can't wait to meet him. And tell Lukas about our grandson."

"Speaking of meeting the baby, Charles, you may go in. But just remember, the delivery tired Chloe. Claire, you may also go in."

Charles rushed towards the bedroom door. He turned to see if Claire would join him. She had sat back down.

"Are you coming?"

"You go in first. I'll come in after the three of you get acquainted."

A few minutes later, Claire met baby Charles Andrew Carter. Or Charlie. They would call him Charlie.

Claire stayed with Chloe for a few days helping her as she recuperated.

On the fourth morning, John called. Emma had gone into labor. Claire torn between staying with Chloe or heading north to John's to help Emma.

"Who was on the telephone, Mama?" Chloe asked as Claire helped her change her nightshirt.

"John. Emma went into labor."

"Oh. Are you going up there?" Chloe hesitantly asked her mother.

"No, not right now. Emma's mama is with her. After the baby comes and I know you are back on your feet." Claire leaned in, squeezed her daughter's shoulders, and said, "I want to stay and help you."

Chloe hemorrhaged after Charlie's birth. It has since subsided, but losing blood weakened her. She tired quickly but showed improvement just that morning.

"Whew!" Chloe sighed. "I need your help. What about Papa?"

"Papa is doing just fine. He survived the week I stayed with Anna Belle. He can survive a week with you. You don't need my help with Charlie. You are taking care of him just fine."

Wah-wah!

A cry from the cradle at the foot of the bed.

"Speaking of Charlie, I guess, he's hungry now," Chloe giggled.

Hours later, John called to say he had a daughter. "Lydia Claire," he told his mama.

"Lydia Claire." Lydia! What a beautiful name! So many new family members to add to her daily prayers. Four babies. Timmy, Elizabeth, Charlie, and Lydia.

Jacob continued to meet with his attorney regularly. Every other week, he walked to the Highland Park Station and took the Ten A.M. to town. He had learned to ignore the whispering and pointing as he passed by the shops. After his meeting, he reversed his trip and hurried back to help on the farms north of town.

The rotating chores worked for some weeks but eventually, it proved tiresome and difficult to coordinate. Jimmy has since moved in to Jacob's house. He experienced a brief encounter with a ranting Lukas one night. Lukas noticed the lights on at Jacob's house and raced over to confront him. He pounded on the door with such force; the walls shook.

As Jimmy opened the door, he saw a clenched fist coming for his face. He quickly ducked and grabbed the forearm to hold the deranged man back.

"Who are you?" they asked in unison.

"Vere's that Jacob at? Vere's does he hide?"

"He's not here. I'm tending to his farm. Who are you?"

"I'm his papa. Who are you?" Jimmy recognized him from the picnic up at his sister's new home.

"Jimmy. Jimmy Tucker." He didn't mention his relations to Emma. He knew better not to elaborate. "I'm working this farm now," he said instead.

"Oh! Jacob's not here?"

"Nope, he's not."

Lukas stood tightlipped. *Where is that boy hiding? Lazy as usual. Not even farming his land.* Lukas thought as he walked away.

Meanwhile, Mrs. Landers had granted permission for Jacob to court Adelaide. Once or twice a week, Jacob trekked to McNally's home for dinner. After dinner, he and Adelaide would sit on a bench behind the house and talk about the future.

The more time he spent with her; the more he realized how perfect she was for him. Adelaide talked about her dreams for a large family living on the lands. Her family had taken trips to Knoxville to visit her ailing grandmother and uncle. She loved that small town.

Like Jacob, Adelaide had grown tired of the stares and whispers. They found her brother not guilty; yet, people still talked.

"I wish I could move away from this area. This used to my town but now I feel like a stranger." Adelaide admitted one night after they had strolled down the street.

Jacob felt the same way.

"I think when this is all over, I might just do that. Move away."

Adelaide's usual bright face saddened. Jacob noticed the difference and said right away, "But not without you."

"Oh, Jacob!" she exclaimed as she leaned in to kiss his cheek.

"Adelaide, until this trial is over, I can't make any promises. If I'm found guilty, I will have to go to jail and wait for an appeal. But if I am found not guilty, I want to take you as far away from here as possible. That is if you will have me?"

"Um…"

"As my wife, Adelaide, I want to marry you when the trial is over. Say yes, please."

"I will. I will marry you."

"But what? No, I haven't asked for permission from your mama and stepfather. I will wait until the trial is over."

"Oh, Jacob, you don't know how long I've waited to hear you say that," she cooed as she flashed a smile and lowered her lids.

"Woman, you need to stop that, or I will forget I am a gentleman and really ruin your reputation." Jacob put his arm around her and pulled her close. He could smell lilacs in her hair as he kissed the top of her head.

Jacob released his hold and quickly started talked about his farm. "I've already talked to Jimmy Tucker, and he has agreed to buy my farm. I'll use the money to pay off my legal fees. And the rest for our future."

Adelaide and Jacob spent the rest of the night talking about their dreams and future.

Please God, they must find him not guilty. I loved him since I was eight. We are meant to be together. Please, please, please, God. Adelaide prayed. Her eyes closed.

Jacob lovingly looked at her angelic face. He thought, *I need to be found not guilty, so I can spend the rest of my life with Adelaide.*

At the end of the summer, Highland Park Church had their last picnic. They invited everyone in Highland Park. The men set up tables that the women filled with fried chicken, breads, and their blue-ribbon pies.

Claire and Lukas attended; and, Chloe and Charles and Anna Belle and Robert. Her daughters proudly pushing their white wicker prams; stopping to allow the women to peek at their sleeping babies.

Lillian arrived with Benjamin after their shifts were over. Benjamin had finished his schooling and was looking at practices outside of Des Moines. Lillian had another year of school but thankfully now, she no longer worked overnight in the wards. Her shifts shorter to allow for more classes and lectures.

William McNally escorted Catherine Landers. Catherine looked radiant in a new dress with his puffy lacey blouse. Her blonder hair fashionably pulled back in a Gibson bun. William smiled; knowing she was his wife now.

After a brief courtship, William proposed to Catherine. They exchanged vows in a quiet ceremony at William's home in front of their families. William's sister and husband traveled down from Ames and along with Catherine's children watched as they professed their love for each other.

Everyone surrounded them at the end of the ceremony. The women hugged Catherine while the men shook William's hand and slapped him on his back to congratulate him for snagging the prettiest widow in Highland Park.

Catherine moved out of her house on Madison Avenue to his large home near his office in Highland Park. Tommy took over their home while Adelaide moved in with Catherine and William. For the first time in her life, Adelaide had her bedroom. She hoped she could sleep without her brother's snoring.

Behind Catherine and William, Adelaide stood; Jacob by her side, carrying a large basket of sweet rolls. The crowd silenced when they saw him. Across the yard, Lukas talked to other farmers as they compared their expected harvests. His back to the crowd. Claire helped set up the tables with the food, she looked up when she heard the fuss and sudden silence. Her face horrified when she realized it was Jacob.

She ran to Jacob's side to warn him. Why did he come? Rumors of his courtship with Adelaide circulated around town. She heard the gossip of Isabelle's father ending his courtship with her after his arrest.

"Catherine!" she called out. "Congratulations," she said to

William as she hugged Catherine. Behind Catherine stood Jacob. She gave him the "What are you doing here" look. Then hugged Adelaide and finally Jacob.

"What are you doing here?" she whispered in his ear. "Your father is sitting right over there."

Meanwhile, Lukas and the other men turned to see if the food was ready. Lukas saw Jacob. His eyes grew angry. He stood up. His fists clenched. He walked across the yard, but another farmer grabbed his arm.

"Lukas, don't. You'll end up in jail."

Lukas turned to look at the man. "That boy killed my son. Do you not understand that? He took my son, my Timmy from me."

"That boy is also your son, Lukas. And he hasn't been convicted yet. He has a right to a trial by a jury."

"He killed my Timmy."

"He hasn't had his day in court," another farmer piped in.

Pastor Griffin stood by the tables; ready to announce it was time to eat. A woman stood by him and held up a cow bell to ring in on his cue. The pastor looked at Lukas then followed his eyes to see Jacob had arrived. He knew he better step in and help the farmers control Lukas.

"Wait," he ordered the woman. With long strides, he stepped in front of Lukas.

"Lukas, we want no trouble here. If you don't think you can take partake peacefully with the meal and games later, then I think you should leave now."

Lukas looked down at his feet. He knew the pastor was right. How could he enjoy himself knowing Jacob sat nearby? Jacob, the one who murdered his son. He murdered my Timmy!

By now, Claire had joined them. Pastor Griffin leaned down and told Claire what he asked Lukas. Claire knew he wouldn't be able to control himself.

Lukas still looked down at the ground. He turned to the pastor and said, "You are right. I must leave."

"Oh, no," Claire said.

"Don't worry, Claire. We will escort you home."

Meanwhile, Lukas walked away. Claire stood and watched him climb into the wagon. But instead of going south; he headed north.

Back to the cemetery, she thought.

Ding-ding-ding!

Pastor Griffin had returned to the tables. "Look, folks, at this delicious spread of food. The Women's Auxiliary have outdone themselves again. After the meal, the competition, err, the games will begin. Tug-of-war, sack races. And I can't remember all the rest. But first, before we eat, we will say prayers, and thank the Lord for providing us with so much. Heavenly Father," he began.

The congregation bowed their heads as they listen to his prayer. When he finished, they all said "Amen."

Claire helped serve food at the buffet table. When the last one went through the line, she made herself a plate. She turned to see the tables full. People busy eating as conversations rose across the yard.

"Mama," she heard.

She looked over to see Jacob standing. "We saved you a seat."

Claire walked over and sat down at their table. By now, Catherine's other children, Michael, Laura, and Tom had arrived. She remembered Catherine's granddaughter, Mollie from Tom's trial. Mollie sat on Tom's lap trying to feed him his meal missing his mouth most of the time. She giggled each time she missed. Mollie adored her uncle and Tom adored Mollie.

Claire sat next Jacob. On his other side, Adelaide. Claire assumed that if they found Jacob not guilty, he and Adelaide would marry.

She caught them looking at each other a time or two during their meal. She always knew they would be together. She remembered another church picnic many years ago. An auction held to raise money for the church. All the young girls, her daughters too, made pies for the auction. A twelve-year-old Jacob paid fifteen cents for Adelaide's apple pie.

After the meal, Adelaide excused herself to visit with her friends, Ethel, Florence, Mabel, and Sadie. She hadn't seen them since she left school a year ago.

"Adelaide!" they exclaimed when she approached them. They ran to greet her. Each hugged Adelaide. Within minutes, they were laughing and talking like they saw each other yesterday.

"We miss you at school."

"I had to go to work. My mama needed the money to pay for Tom's attorney fees."

"I heard your mama married that attorney. What's his name?"

"William McNally. Mama is happy again. Like she was before my papa died. As much as I remember. I was just six."

"That's wonderful. Did you mama stop working at the college?"

"Mama is determined she will pay all of Tom's fees. William told mama she didn't have to pay anymore, but she says she owes him."

Mabel looked over at the table where Catherine sat. Catherine and William engrossed in a conversation with Claire Johansson. She couldn't see who sat next to Mrs. Johansson.

"Who else is sitting with you? Gracie's' papa?"

"No, Jacob."

"Jacob. Jacob Johansson. Fess up, Adelaide!"

"Jacob and I are courting."

"Oooohhh!" the girls cooed.

"What about his, uh?"

"His trial. I'm praying a lot."

"But Adelaide, what will you do if,"

"I'm trying not to think about that because when I do, I cry."

Adelaide's eyes teared up.

"Oh, Adelaide, we did not want to upset you."

"I have loved Jacob since fifth grade. We are meant to be together. Forever," Adelaide sighed and placed her hands over her heart.

"Everyone knew you had a crush on Jacob. I remember Grace saying how it would be great to have you as her sister-in-law."

The school friends lowered their head as they remembered their friend, Grace.

"Has Jacob asked for your hand yet?" Sadie asked changing the subject.

"No, he has not asked my mama or my stepfather, but we have talked about our future. We must wait until after the trial. My mama said I can go back to school now, but I will stay working to save money."

"Save for what??" Florence asked curiously.

"Oh, nothing," Adelaide replied. She didn't want to reveal their secret plans. Plans only Adelaide and Jacob knew.

"I better get back to my family."

The girls hugged each other. Adelaide turned around and walked back to the table. Jacob looked up as she approached the table. He winked at her and her heart fluttered. She smiled.

* * * * * * * * *

Jacob sat alone on a bench waiting for the trolley. The trial would start next week. He hoped the trolley would be there soon as he wanted to stop at the diner for a quick meal before he walked back to the Tucker farm. He needed to see Adelaide's sweet face. See that smile that drove him crazy and hear her soft voice.

Earlier today, he remembered more about that night. He remembered walking down the path towards Poor Farm Rd. But that was it.

He recalled waking up the next morning. His body ached, a new tear on his shirt and a few scratches on his face and arms. He remembered trying to use the old water pump behind the house; surprised to find the lever missing.

He remembered walking home and washing at the pump behind the farmhouse before walk inside. He used the front hoping his parents were in the back of the house, so he could sneak up to his room.

CHAPTER 18

November 2, 1903

Claire raced to keep up with Lukas. Another murder trial to endure but this time it was their own son. Conflicted, Claire's thoughts raced. She wanted the Police to solve the murders of her children, but she anguished over her part in her son's arrest.

For the past six months, Grace fretted over her accusation. She regretted telling Pastor Griffin.

What was she thinking? She didn't think he would go to the police. She confided in her pastor. That's it.

For months, a rift separated Claire from her son. Jacob said nothing, but his actions confirmed her fears. He knew it was her. Finally, at the church picnic, she had her chance. Adelaide stepped away to visit with her former school friends. Catherine and William engrossed in their own conversation.

"Jacob," Claire said.

Jacob turned and looked at his mama. "Yes, mama.'

Clare's eyes welted as she began her apology. She told him how she sorry she was. She apologized for not being able to help him. And she told him how she prayed for years he would court a fine woman who would love and care for him. And now she prayed for his acquittal.

Jacob accepted her apology. He told her God answered her prayers; that Adelaide made him happy and they would marry after the trial. But he didn't tell her their plans to leave the area. That secret belonged to Adelaide and him.

She had made amends with Jacob. He forgave her. That's all that counted. Now she prayed his attorney would win this trial.

Inside the courthouse, the same man sat with his newspaper open across the desk.

"Johansson trial," Lukas asked.

"Courtroom two."

The same room, Claire thought. The same courtroom as Tommy Landers.

Claire followed Lukas up the massive stairs. At the top, they both walked around the atrium until they reached the double doors that read "COURTROOM TWO" in black block letters.

Lukas opened one door and Claire stepped inside. She made her way to the bench behind the District Attorney. Josiah Jones sat at the table this time. To his right, Peter Culligan. With his hands folded in his lap, he resembled a boy who mother reprimanded him; not an attorney. Culligan had lost the first trial and the district attorney didn't want another not guilty verdict.

Robert Hammil sat on the other side. His notes in front of him. He knew this was a huge stepping stone for his career.

Claire and Lukas took the same seats from the earlier trial. Claire looked around the room. Nothing had changed. The same imposing painting of Roosevelt watched over the room. The judge's desk in the middle; the red, white, and blue flag to the left.

In the jury box, the twelve jurors sat quietly. The men, all bearded, came from neighborhoods all over Des Moines. No jurors lived in Highland Park area. Claire recognized none of the men but swore they were the same men from Tom Landers' trial.

Claire heard the door close behind them. She turned to see her son, John and her daughters, Chloe, and Anna Belle. They walked up the aisle but instead of turning towards Claire; they went the other way. They sat on the other side. They came to support their brother.

John glanced at his mother before he sat down. Claire looked directly into John's eyes. Without saying a word, she let him know. She understood and approved. Lukas turned to see who had arrived too.

"Why are they sitting over there? He's a murderer. He killed my boy,' Lukas asked.

"Jacob is also their brother."

"They are traitors. They are no longer welcome in my home."

"You don't mean that. We raised them to be compassionate adults. That family comes first."

"Timmy was their family too."

"You forget about Grace. That hurts my heart you don't mourn for Grace; only Timmy."

"Ja, ja. Grace too."

The sound of a door closing interrupted their conversation. Lillian, escorted by Benjamin, walked in, and sat down next to Claire. She too, noticed the division of the family.

"Mama! Why are they sitting over there?"

"They came to support Jacob."

"But, mama, he killed Grace and Timmy."

"Lil, he hasn't been found guilty yet."

Across the aisle, Chloe whispered to John, "Papa doesn't look happy we are sitting here."

"No, he doesn't but Mama understands."

"How do you know?"

"I just know."

Chloe pried for more information, but John just repeated his comments. He held up his hand to stop her questions and said, "Trust me, I know she understands."

Behind them, the seats had filled. Chloe turned to see Jacob's friends, David, and Harry, seated near the back. They would testify for defense. John's father-in-law, George Tucker, sat alone in the back. He came to support Jacob. Working side by side, the two became close; a father-son relationship. He agreed to be a character witness for Jacob.

On the other side, Dr. Baker and Pastor Griffin sat directly behind Claire and Lukas. Detective Maloney and Officer Morrow sat in the last row. A few reporters sat next to the police officers while friends and neighbors filled in the remaining seats.

Just before ten o'clock, Adelaide Landers slipped in. She sat in the back row, but Anna Belle motioned for her to sit with them. Reserved for the defendant's family, a chair sat empty in the front row. As Adelaide walked up the center aisle to the front, she heard the gasps and whispers.

They wonder why I would court a murderer! Jacob is innocent. They don't know Jacob like I do. They don't love him like I do.

Adelaide took her seat and nervously smiled at Anna Belle.

"Thank you," she whispered.

"You are family. And important to Jacob."

Conversations filled the courtroom as neighbors greeted neighbors, the reporters shared information and district attorneys discussed their case.

The galley silenced as the side door opened and Jacob entered the room. Dressed in a white-collared shirt and black pants and his face clean-shaven, they barely recognized him, Behind him, the bailiff. Jacob looked at his siblings. They sensed his fear. The next weeks would decide his life. His eyes softened when he saw Adelaide.

Jacob winked. Adelaide sighed. Anna Belle smiled. Her brother was smitten. Anna Belle reached over. She grabbed Adelaide's hand and squeezed it.

Adelaide closed her eyes and prayed. Her eyes filled with tears. A lone tear flowed down her cheek. She reached up to wipe it away. She needed to be strong. She couldn't let Jacob, or his family know her fear.

Robert Hammil leaned over and whispered into Jacob's ear. Jacob nodded.

"All rise, the Honorable Emmet Cooper residing," the bailiff yelled out.

The entire courtroom stood.

Emmet Cooper walked out of his chambers and climbed the steps to the bench. He surveyed the courtroom before he sat down. Lifting his gavel, he slammed it down onto the table and sat down.

"Please take a seat," the judge said.

"Iowa Criminal Courts is now in session," the bailiff said.

"This is the trial of the State of Iowa versus James Jacob Johansson. Mr. Johansson, you are charged with the murders of Grace Claire Johansson and Timothy Lukas Johansson, how do you plead?"

Jacob stood next to his attorney. His heart pounded, his palms sweaty.

"No-not guilty, your honor." His voiced cracked as he spoke.

Across the room, Lukas mumbled loudly. The judge, aware of Lukas' outbursts, addressed the situation before the trial started.

"Ladies and Gentlemen in the galley. I will have no talking, yelling, clapping, or cheering during this trial or I will remove you." The last part directed at Lukas.

Lukas tightened his lips, folded his arms across his chest and glared back at the judge.

The judge looked down at the paper in front of him. "I trust you are both prepared for the trial."

"Yes, Your Honor," Robert Hammill replied.

"Yes, sir," Josiah Jones said as he stood up.

"You may begin."

Hammill took his seat as Jones walked to the podium facing the jury. He placed his book down in front of him and cleared his throat.

"Gentlemen of the jury. On April 13, 1902, Grace Johansson and her brother Timothy attended Sunday evening service. A service they attended every week. Timmy earned a nickel working on the family farm and they stopped with their friend for some coconut candy. Timmy shared the candy and the rest they would share with their family at home. But the never made it home. Just one thousand feet from their front door, someone attacked them. Someone beat them and left to die on the side of the road. The coconut candy spread out on the gravel road. Along blood droplets, hair and brain matter."

Jones paused.

"The State will present evidence that implicates that man," he turned and pointed at Jacob.

"That man, James Johansson, is responsible for the murders of Grace and Timothy. Yes, Jacob, as he is known, murdered his own brother and sister. He murdered his brother. A brother he shared a room with for thirteen years. Who slept in the bed next to his, every night. Until his death. A brother who worked side by side in the evening milking the cows. He murdered his sister who dreamed of faraway places. A sister who would be the first to receive a high school education. A girl aspiring to be a writer. Her whole life a head of her."

The district attorney paused again.

"Jacob Johansson is an angry man. In a jealous rage, he beat his brother and sister to death. He dragged and threw their bloody beaten bodies into the ditch. Their family asleep just one thousand feet away; in fact, in a home visible from the murder site."

"In the days that followed, Mr. Johansson joined his family at the visitation. He stood in church and listened to their pastor eulogize his siblings. He stood at the cemetery and watched them lower their caskets into ground. He watched his parents grieve, his sisters heartbroken, his brother mournful. But did he care, no? He continued with his life. He moved into his own home, courted a young lady in town and prepared for his future. Like nothing ever happened."

"He didn't shed a tear. He didn't shed a tear because he wanted his brother gone. And poor Grace, she got in the way. He didn't shed a tear."

Jones closed the book in front of him and looked back up.

"Thank you."

Jones stepped away from the podium. He walked back to his

seat and sat down. His eyes scanned the jury box. Their faces melancholy.

The judge turned towards Robert Hammil and nodded.

Hammil stood, scooped up his papers and walked towards the podium. He placed his papers down and took a deep breath.

"Good morning, gentlemen," he started. "I can't deny that the murders of these two innocent children wasn't horrific. That whoever committed the murder should be held accountable. Punished for their crime. But the police haven't caught the murderer yet. It was not Jacob Johansson. I am prepared to present evidence that Jacob had no hand in the deaths of his sister and brother. That night, like most nights, Jacob joined his friends at that river banks for comradery. The men talked about local events, the news, even baseball. They discussed new inventions and their futures. His friends will testify that night they shared whiskey and like many a young man, Jacob indulged too much and needed help home. They will testify that he couldn't walk and passed out as soon as they got him home."

Jacob looked down; embarrassed at his actions and afraid to look at Adelaide.

"The prosecutor bases his case on hunches, feelings, but no evidence. There is no evidence Jacob committed the murder, no evidence placing him at the scene. Nothing. No witnesses, no blood-stained clothing, nothing that implicates him."

"Yes, gentlemen of the jury, nothing. Absolutely nothing." He paused for a few seconds, then said, "Thank you."

When he had seated, Judge Cooper looked over at the prosecutor and said, "Please call your first witness."

"The prosecution calls Detective Maloney."

"Detective Maloney," the bailiff bellowed.

Detective Maloney stood and holding his hat in his hands, walked up to the witness box. The bailiff stood in front holding the Bible.

"Place your left hand on the Bible and raise your right hand," he instructed the detective. "Do you swear to tell the truth, the whole truth and nothing but the truth so help you, God?" he asked.

"I do."

"You may take a seat."

As the detective sat down in the witness box, Josiah Jones stood up.

"Please state your full name."

"George Albert Maloney."

"Thank you. Please share your occupation."

"I am a detective with the Des Moines Police Department stationed at the Highland Park Precinct. I have been with the department for fifteen years and a detective for the last five years."

"And you were the arresting officer?

"Yes, I was."

"Can you describe the scene you found that night?"

Maloney began, "I arrived at the scene on Madison

Avenue. The bodies removed and at the undertakers. With lanterns, we could see drag trails and blood droppings on the gravel. The next morning, it is evident that the children died a brutal death. The grass in the ditches covered in blood. Candy scattered all over the roadway."

"And the cause of death?"

"Someone beat them to death."

"Is this the weapon that used to commit the murders?" Jones asked holding up a pipe.

"Yes, we believe it to be."

"And how did you come to receive it?"

"A young boy brought it to us. He said a man gave it to him."

"And the other man was?"

"Jacob, I mean, James Johansson."

"The defendant? Mr. Johansson gave the pipe to this young boy and?"

"He told this young lad, Robbie Richardson, to take it to the police."

"Do you know where the pipe was found?"

"We have an approximate location. They found the pipe in the fields across from the Johansson farm and close to the farmhouse owned by the defendant."

"Is the blood human blood?"

"Yes, we had it tested at Drake University and they determined it to be human blood. And a few strands of human hair too."

"Is there any other evidence that implicates the defendant?"

"Everyone knows Jacob and his father were at odds. Rumors circulated that Lukas changed his will giving all of his property to Timothy."

"Objection, hearsay!" Hammil stood and bellowed.

"I agree," the judge said. "Please concentrate on the evidence and not rumors, Mr. Jones."

"Yes, your honor. Detective, was the defendant a suspect before his arrest?"

"Yes, sir. A good detective looks at everyone when solving a murder. Family members included. All the Johansson family were suspects but one by one we crossed them off. Only Jacob remained on the brief list of suspects."

"No more questions."

* * * * * * * * *

At Mrs. O'Leary's boarding house, the young man buttoned up his shirt. It made well, but he felt guilty about wearing it.

It was just a year ago; he recalled. He sat on his bed in front looking at the logs burning in the fireplace. His shirt balled up in his hands. He remembered standing up and tossing the shirt into the flames. The fire roared. He watched it burn in the fire until not a thread remained.

Mrs. O'Leary laundered his clothes as part of his rent. A few weeks later, she handed him his folded clothing and said, "I couldn't help noticing that one of your shirts is missing. Did you need me to make you another one? I can do it for fifty cents." He remembered that conversation like it was yesterday and not over a year ago.

CHAPTER 19

Robert Hammil stood up.

"Detective, can you describe what you saw at the scene?"

"By the time I arrived, both of the victims were taken to the funeral home. It was still dark, but you could tell something horrifying happened there. At sunrise, I could see more. There was blood spattered all over the gravel, the drag marks to either side had blood in it. Yes, just a lot of blood around. In the ditch."

"With all the blood spatter, do you think it would cover the killer with blood?"

"Yes, they would."

"Did you find any bloody clothes of Jacob's?

"No, but it was a year before we arrested him."

"But did you not say you suspected all the family members from the beginning?"

"Yes, but we didn't search their house."

"But why not?"

"The family held the funerals, and we were looking at a lot of others suspects too."

"Were their other arrests?" he asked knowing the answer.

"Yeah, we arrested another man."

"And they tried him and found him not guilty."

"Yes, that is correct."

"Was there anymore?"

"No charges filed, but we detained a negro coal miner."

"And you released him?"

"Yes, we confirmed his whereabouts at the time of the murders."

"You detained one man, arrested another who found not guilty and now you have a third man. Is that correct?"

"Yes."

"Did you look outside the Highland Park area or Des Moines? Or even Iowa?"

"I sent Telegraphs to all cities along the train route."

"Did you receive any response?"

"Just one. Someone reported two men lurking around in Burlington."

"Were they questioned? Detained?"

"Yes, by the local police. They said they came from Ohio. Hadn't made it to Des Moines area."

"What else did you do?"

"We solicited the public's help. Received a lot of possible suspects."

Hamill walked over to the table and picked up a bound book.

"Is this the book of possible leads?"

"Yes, it is."

"Let me read a few. We have a man drunk every night and doesn't remember what he does. A stranger approached a woman walking near Madison Ave. Nasty neighbors, unknown men, coal miners, and so and so on. Were any of these men detained?"

"No, I reviewed the details and determined they weren't viable suspects."

"No other investigation. You didn't even look for them."

"We had other suspects."

"Oh, yes, the two other men. One detained and released. The other tried and found not guilty. So, after that trial, you set your sights on the brother?"

"He was someone we considered a person of interest."

"But you arrested Tom, Tom Landers?"

"Yes."

"Why?"

"The pipe. A pipe was missing from their water pump."

"Anything else?"

"He had a crush on Grace."

"I see. And now Jacob is on trial. What was the reason?"

"He found the pipe, but he didn't bring it in."

"Has the murderer ever provide you with the weapon?"

"I have investigated no other murders. I don't think that happens. The person would have to be touched."

"Insane?"

"Yep, most likely."

"Wouldn't the suspect try to get rid the weapon?"

"Yeah."

Jones slipped his fingers in his shirt collar. He felt the trial slipping through his fingers.

"Are you familiar with the Capital Hill Thug in Denver, Colorado?"

"I read a bulletin about that case. Don't recall the details. It was a few years ago. I believe, it remains unsolved."

"Are you aware that all the victims were beaten?"

"Like I said, I don't recall the details."

"Did you know some victims were on their way home from Sunday night church service?"

"No, don't remember that."

"With a steel pipe?"

"I don't recall."

"Does that sound familiar"

"Yes, it does, sir."

"Let me provide you with the details since you don't recollect. Someone attacked eleven victims in Denver. The last attack was Summer of 1901. Eight months later, the children are attacked in Iowa. The Denver police believe the attacker has left the state. What do you think? Could the Capital Hill Thug have been in Iowa?"

"Uh, uh, um. Yes, I imagine he could. But…"

"No further questions," he said interrupting the detective.

"But…"

"No further questions," Hamill bellowed.

The judge looked at the detective and said, "You may step down."

The dejected detective stood up and walked back to his seat. He looked over at the district attorney and tried to apologize with his eyes, but Jones just shook his head in disbelief.

Jones stood and said, "The prosecutor calls Dr. Frederick Baker."

After the doctor acknowledged the oath, the district attorney stood and walked to the podium.

"Dr. Baker, will you please tell us what happened on the night of the thirteenth of April?"

"Around ten-fifteen, Isaac Swan knocked on my door. He said he and three other men found the bodies of the children. I telephoned the police, grabbed my bag, and headed out the door. Since he said there were two victims, I suggested we stop and get another doctor. Dr. Williams lives down the road a bit, so we got him and hurried to the scene. There we found the children. Timmy, the male was on the north side. They beat his face so bad I didn't recognize him."

"I examined the male, and he was still alive. I knew we had to get him to the hospital right away. The ambulance arrived, and we put both victims in the back. I climbed in and examined both and the female was deceased. The male was still breathing, but it was labored. I tried to find out who did this, but he didn't respond."

Dr. Baker could see Claire and Lukas from his seat. Wanting to spare them from hearing more gory details of their child's death, he said, "Shortly after the ambulance started, the male stopped breathing."

"What happened the next day?"

"I performed an autopsy to determine the cause of death; but it was they obvious someone bludgeoned them to death."

"And their injuries?"

Dr. Baker explained the injuries they sustained. Every broken bone. Every bruise. Every bloody laceration.

He finished with "We believe a blunt object caused the injuries."

"Thank you, Dr. Baker." He turned to the judge and said, "No further questions."

The judge looked towards the other table and said, "Your witness."

Robert Hammil waited a minute before standing. He had watched the jury during the entire testimony. He walked to the podium knowing his work cut out for him.

"Dr. Baker, you describe the scene as bloody. Did you have any blood on your clothing after examining the victims?"

"I examined the male and yes, my clothes had blood on them. My pants where I knelt next to Timmy. My shirt from cradling his head to examine it. My hands. There was blood all over the road."

"And the children's clothing?"

"Obviously, it covered them. Their clothing splattered with their own blood too."

"With all that blood, do you think the killer would have gotten blood on his clothing?"

"I don't see how he couldn't."

"No further questions."

Hammil took his seat. He put his hand on Jacob's shoulder and gave it squeeze. In his eyes, he had accomplished doubt in the prosecutor's case.

Across the aisle, Jones contemplated his next witness. It was time for a sympatric witness.

"The State calls Claire Johansson."

"Claire Johansson," the bailiff bellowed.

Claire gracefully walked to the witness box and turned towards the bailiff. She lifted her right hand and placed her left on the Bible.

"I do," she said then sat down.

"Good morning, Mrs. Johansson."

"Good morning, Mr. Jones."

"Mrs. Johansson, do you remember the morning after they found your children?

"I do. Lukas, my husband, and I sat in the parlor the whole night. I don't think we closed our eyes to sleep the whole night. I was still in disbelief and prayed for answers from God. When morning broke, I knew we would have to tell the other children. Lukas wanted to tend to the milking. I stopped him and told him Daniel, our hired hand could take on the cows. And Jacob too. When I went upstairs, Jacob was not in his bed."

"Any chance he could have left before that?"

"His bed was made. And we didn't sleep at all. I would have heard him coming down the stairs."

"Go on."

"I ran down the stairs and told Lukas that Jacob wasn't at home. I feared something happened to him too. Lukas said he probably had drunk too much. And then the door opened, and Jacob walked in."

"How did Jacob look?"

"Bloodshot eyes, his hair a mess, alcohol on his breath. His clothes dirty and dusty."

"Anything else?"

"He had a tear in his shirt. A new one."

"How did he react when you told him about Grace and Timmy?"

"He didn't. My husband had to repeat it."

"Did he look surprised?"

"No, he didn't."

"Did he say anything?"

"He said I'm sorry."

"Anything else?"

"He said he would milk the cows. And went to the barn. Afterwards, he loaded up the milk cans and took them to the creamery."

"Did you find that unusual?"

"Not then. But after the funeral I thought it was strange."

"Strange enough to think he could be the killer?"

Claire looked directly at the district attorney. She could feel her families' eyes staring at her. She couldn't look at Jacob at that moment.

Claire whispered, "Yes."

"I'm sorry. Could you repeat that?"

"Yes, I did."

The galley gasped at her acknowledgement.

"No further questions."

Mr. Hammil stood up. He had never met Jacob's mother or father and wished he had met them in different circumstances.

"Mrs. Johansson," he said as he nodded. "You stated that Jacob's clothes were dusty and dirty. Can you tell me what he did during the day?

"He farmed. He helped my husband with the farm. And milk the cows too."

"What do you mean, helping with the farm?"

"Plowing, fixing fences, cleaning barns."

"Would he get dirty during the day?"

"Oh, yes. I had to wash his clothing several times a week."

"Did he ever tear his clothes working the farm?"

"Always. He would catch it on the plow or a fence. Oh, my, I was always mending his shirts."

"Would you say you were familiar with his clothing?"

"Yes. I am still. I was. I washed them often. I mended them. I sewed his shirts, too."

"Would it be unusual for Jacob to come home with a dirty ripped shirt?"

"Well, no. It happened often in the spring when they would fix fences or replacing missing planks after the winter. Or working in the fields."

"Jacob lived in your home for three or four months after the murders. Am I correct?"

"Yes, he did until his house was ready."

"Did you notice any of clothing missing after that night?"

"Nothing was missing. He owned just three shirts and two pants plus his church shirt and pants, but he wouldn't wear those to work on the farm."

"How long after you washed his clothing were ready to wear?"

"In winter, I hung them in the kitchen by the stove to dry. It took hours for them to dry. Sometimes the entire day. In warmer months, they hung outside and dried quicker if it was sunny and hot but almost all day if it was cloudy."

"How about at ten o'clock at night?"

"Unless someone kept a fire going. They could still be damp."

"You said earlier that Jacob's clothing was dirty and torn that morning following the murder, am I correct?"

"Yes, I said that."

"When you saw Jacob that morning, did he have any blood on his clothing?"

"No, I don't recall blood on his clothes."

"Were they damp like they been washed?"

"No, they were dirty and dusty."

"Did Jacob know how to wash his clothes?"

"That was the girls' chores. He would have carried buckets of hot water to washtub. But never scrub the clothes clean."

"When you told him about the murders, did he say anything else?"

"Yes, he told his papa to stay with me and he would milk the cows."

"Is milking the cows necessary?"

"The cows have to milk twice a day, or they could dry up."

"Was your farm a dairy or crop farm?"

"Lukas was converting the farm from dairy to crop."

"Did you need the income from the milk?"

"Yes, we sold our milk to the creamery in town. The one that Jacob worked for."

"Is it possible that Jacob's working was just him being responsible?"

"Jacob was very responsible. He worked for the creamery for going on five years."

"Thank you, Mrs. Johansson. No further questions."

Hammil returned to his seat as Claire left the witness stand. Behind him, John pitied his mother. He didn't like Hammil's questioning his mama but knew, for Jacob's sake, it was necessary.

Jacob's eyes followed his mother as she stood and walked back to her seat. Hammil did his job. Instead of looking like a crazed killer, Jacob came off "smelling like roses."

Josiah Jones contemplated his next move. An attorney must tread lightly when questioning the victims' mother. Badgering that witness could prove detrimental to the defendant. Hammil blended a perfect combination of tough questions and defendant sympathy.

Jones looked at the clock on the wall. About noon. *I better call my next witness and fix this at once.*

Jones half stood to call the next witness when he heard a loud bang. The judge slammed down his gavel.

"We will recess until one o'clock."

The district attorney's heart sunk. The worse possible scenario ending on a positive for the defendant. They would spend his lunch planning the afternoon session's an uphill battle.

Behind him, the crowd made their way out of the courtroom. Hammil and Jacob followed his siblings down the aisle. John and his sisters discussed where to eat.

When the last person had left the courtroom, Jones turned to the man sitting next to him and said, "Well, Culligan, we have a lot of work to do over lunch."

Culligan agreed as he scooped up the documents on the table, thankful he packed a sandwich and fruit that morning.

Meanwhile, outside, Jacob moved to stand next to Adelaide and casually brushed her arm. She turned and flashed him a smile.

That smile melted his heart.

After a light lunch, the family returned to the courthouse. John held open the door for the women. Adelaide hesitated before entering the building.

Jacob, who stood behind her, sensed her fear. He leaned down and whispered near her ear, "Soon, this will be behind us and we can get on with our lives."

Feeling his breath on her neck sent chills up her spine. Adelaide nodded and walked into the building.

As they walked in the courtroom, they saw a little boy and his mother sitting in the back row. A key witness for the prosecution, Robbie Richardson would give testimony that Josiah Jones thought would turn the trial in his favor.

The judge took his seat at the head of the room and the afternoon session began.

The state called Robbie Richardson to the stand. Robbie stood right up and walked up the aisle. He stopped in front of the bailiff and said, "Aren't ya goin' to ask me that question? I know what to say this time. Go ahead."

The bailiff held out the bible. Robbie put his hand on the Bible and raised his right hand. When the bailiff finished, he said, "I do."

Robbie jumped up in the witness chair, looked over at the judge and said, "I'm ready."

Laughter spread throughout the galley.

Jones stood up. "Can you state your name for the courts?"

"Well, like I said the last time, my name is John Robert Richardson, but it's my papa's name too. My mama and papa call me Robbie. Oh, and my grandma and gramps. And my cousins, and aunts and uncles."

"Everybody calls you Robbie?"

"Not my teachers. I'm Robert in school."

"Good. How old are you?"

"I am nine."

"Do you remember that day someone gave you the pipe?"

"Uh-uh."

"Is that a yes?"

"Oh, yeah, yes, I do."

"I was walkin' home from school right past where the kids who died lived an' this man came out of the fields.' He had the pipe in his hand, and I ran cuz I wus scared. An' he told me to stop; that he wasn't goin' to hurt me. 'N I stopped. He said he found the pipe, but he didn't have anee' time to take it to the Police. He asked me if I would take it. And I ran all the way there."

"Thank you, Robbie. Now, I will ask a question and I need you to just answer yes or no."

Robbie nodded.

"Robbie, do you see the man who gave the pipe in this courtroom today?"

"Yes," Robbie answered firmly.

"Now I will ask you to point to the man who gave you the pipe."

Robbie raised his arm and with his index finger, he pointed towards Jacob.

"This man here," Jones asked walked over to the defendants. He stopped in front of Jacob and held out his hand. "This man."

"That's him, I mean, yes."

"Thank you, Robbie," Jones said, then turned toward Hamill and added, "Your witness."

Hamill stood up and walked over towards Robbie.

"Robbie, when that man came out of the fields, were you scared?"

"At first, I was but then when he told me he wasn't goin' to hurt me, I wasn't anymore. He wus nice to me."

"You didn't think he would hurt you?"

"Nah, he wus nice. He said he didn't have time and I should take it to the police station. I ran all the way there."

"Thank you, Robbie. You have been very helpful."

"You're welcome, sir."

Hamill returned to his seat. The bailiff walked over towards the witness stand.

"I can step down now?" Robbie asked.

The bailiff smiled and nodded. Robbie jumped down and ran back to his mama. They quickly exited the courtroom.

CHAPTER 20

The rest of the day, the prosecutor called one witness after another. Pastor Griffin said everyone knew about the rift between Lukas and Jacob. Hamill asked how he knew there were issues. The pastor responded with "Everybody knew it."

"Are you saying it is gossip?"

"Uh, not exactly."

"Is it a fact? Did Lukas or Jacob tell you of their problems?"

"No, they didn't tell me. I knew."

"How?"

"They never sat next to each other at Sunday Service."

"How did they sit?"

"Lukas was always on the aisle, Claire usually sat next to him and then the other children next to Claire. Timmy usually was next to his mother, then the girls and Jacob on the side. John sat there too before he got married."

"Did Lukas have a rift with all of his children?"

"No, not at all. Not that I heard."

"What exactly does the Bible say about gossiping?"

"It encourages people not to gossip." The pastor hung his head in shame.

"One more question, Pastor. Mrs. Johansson told you in confidence she knew who the killer was, am I correct?"

"Yes, she did."

"Did she have solid evidence or was it a hunch?"

"It was a hunch."

"I need to verify this conversation. Mrs. Johansson told you she thought Jacob did it, had no evidence or knowledge of the murders and you went to the police with this information, correct?"

"Yes, but."

Hammil interrupted him. "Thank you, Pastor. No further questions."

"The State calls Lillian Johansson."

Chloe and Anna Belle looked at each other confused. "Why is Lillian testifying?" Chloe whispered to her sister. Anna Belle just shook her head.

Lillian walked up to the front of the courtroom. After taking the oath, she sat down.

Josiah Jones walked up to the podium. "Miss Johansson? How are you related to the victims?"

"Grace and Timmy were my younger sister and brother."

"And the defendant?"

"He is my brother. One of my brothers."

"Did you attend the private funeral service held at the funeral home?"

"Yes, I did. With my family."

'Did your family each say their final goodbyes in the privacy of the funeral home?"

"Yes, we all went up. First my Grandmother and Great-Aunt. Then my sisters' and their beaus. Then Jacob and I."

"Can you tell me what happened when you were saying your final farewell to Grace?"

"Yes, I leaned in a kissed Grace's cheek. Then Jacob walked up."

"What did Jacob do?"

"He leaned down and whispered."

"What did he say?"

"He whispered I'm sorry."

"I'm sorry."

"What do you think he meant?"

"Objection!" Hammil bellowed.

"Sustained," the judge replied. "Please ask a question the witness can answer."

Jones looked down at his notes as he tried to rephrase his question. He needed Lillian to answer this question.

Finally, he asked, "What did you think when he said that?"

"I didn't believe it. I turned to see if any of my family heard him."

"What did you do after that?"

"We said our goodbyes to Timmy."

"What did you do?"

"The same as I did with Grace. Kissed Timmy and said "goodbye."

"And Jacob?"

"He leaned down towards Timmy and whispered something, but I didn't hear what he said."

"Thank you, Miss Johansson."

Hammil walked up to the podium. He placed his notebook on the podium and cleared his throat.

"Miss Johansson, good morning."

"Good morning, Mr. Hammil."

"You said Jacob whispered something to Grace."

"Yes, he whispered I'm sorry."

"How clear was it?"

"It was quiet. You could hear a pin drop."

"Is it possible that Jacob was just sorry that this happened to her?"

"Well, I guess it is possible."

"And you said you didn't hear what Jacob whispered to Timmy?"

"Yes, I did."

"Is there a chance he might have said the same thing to Timmy?"

"I, um, I, I, I, well, I'm not sure."

In the galley, John smiled to himself. Nothing shook Lillian. She was tough, but Hammil made her stumble. He felt good about Jacob's chances of an acquittal.

The next witness, Johansson's hired hand, Daniel, testified to Jacob's demeanor the morning after the murders. He also said Jacob knew of his father's intent to give the farm to Timmy. On cross-examining, Daniel admitted that only part of the farm would go to Timmy as Claire owned the property where their home and outbuildings stood and the fields across Madison Ave. Lukas owned the acres on the other side of Poor Farm Road.

The district attorney's heart sunk after that testimony. His whole case based on the premise that Jacob killed his brother, so he could inherit the whole farm.

One by one, Hammil tore apart his case. Jones shook his head in despair; his strongest witness was a nine-year-old boy.

Jones stood up and said the words he would regret, "The prosecution rests."

The judge looked up at the clock on the wall. Half past four. Too late to start another witness.

"We will convene at nine a.m. sharp tomorrow. Court is dismissed." With a bang of the gavel, he stood and walked out of the room.

John and his sister rose and turned towards the center aisle. On the other side, Lillian, Claire, and Lukas stood and made their way to the aisle. The divided family met in the aisle. Adelaide in the middle.

Lukas mumbled, "They are dead to me. Dead as my boy."

Claire turned him and said, "This is not the time and place to air our dirty laundry."

Outside, Claire and Lukas walked north to catch the Highland Park trolley. Lillian and Ben walked east towards the river to catch the Riverside trolley. Not wanting to share the same trolley as their parents, the others stayed back at the courthouse to catch the later train.

Hammil talked to Jacob off to the side.

"Jacob," he started. "Jacob, I believe this is going well for us. Tomorrow, the prosecution will rest. And I will call on your witnesses. Will David and Harry be here in the morning?"

"Yes, sir. They have been here every day."

"Good, son, good. Get a good night's rest. I will see you in the morning."

"Will do. Thank you."

Hammil turned and walked toward his office. He had a lot of preparations for tomorrow. His wife wouldn't expect him home. His extra suit hung on the coat rack in the reception area. A blanket and feather pillow on the sofa in the corner of his office.

John and his sisters walked ahead; while Jacob and Adelaide followed them. Jacob placed his hand on her elbow. Adelaide felt the warmth of his skin making it difficult for her to concentrate. She tripped on a raised stone.

Jacob reached his arm around her waist to steady her. She turned to face him.

Adelaide looked up at Jacob and shyly smiled. Jacob looked down at her pretty face. He so badly wanted to kiss her but resisted the urge. There were too many nosy people around.

Finally, he said, "My attorney says it's going well for us. Tomorrow, he will call on John, David, and Harry. And Mr. Tucker. And you, too. Are you ready?"

"Yes, Jacob," Adelaide whispered.

"Adelaide, please don't look at me like that. I want to kiss you."

Adelaide stopped smiling but the love she had for Jacob showed in her eyes. She continued, "When will jury convene?"

"The day after. The shorter they take to decide, the better for me. And you. And we can start our life together. I have a judge ready to meet us after the verdict."

"Oh, Jacob, I am so scared. I have waited all my life to be with you and I am afraid I'm going to lose you."

"You won't. My attorney said it's going well." Jacob lowered his voice so only Adelaide could hear him and said, "Darling, we will be together. Finally."

"Finally," Adelaide said exhaling.

Chloe turned to see if they were still behind her. She heard bits and pieces of the conversation behind her. She smiled to herself. Her brother was in love.

CHAPTER 21

Earlier that morning, David and Harry hurried to the courtroom. As witnesses for the defense, they would be the first ones called to testify.

David thought about the night. Even though it was a year ago, he remembered every detail. Jacob drank too much. Harry had a bottle of homemade whiskey. The kind of hooch that burned your throat going down. But after the second or third swig, you didn't notice.

He remembered Jacob showing up a little late that night. They could see the anger in Jacob's eyes. He grunted a hello and sat down on a rock before asking for the whiskey. David looked at Harry as he passed the bottle to Jacob. Jacob took a long drink; stopping only to cough. "That shit will choke ya!" he said before raising the bottle to his lips again. He drank three or four swigs before passing it back to Harry. Soon after, Jacob ranted, his words slurred as he complained about his father, he swayed back and forth on the rock. David feared he would hurt himself.

By eight o'clock, Jacob's condition worsened. His head lowered as he struggled to stay upright.

"Ima goin' take care uv it now," Jacob slurred as he stood to leave. He stopped for just a minute to catch his balance before he turned to climb the bank. Afraid he might fall over and hit his head on one the rocks, David suggested they walk him home.

Jacob staggered up the river bank and tripped on a large rock. Harry reached down to help him up ripping his shirt as Jacob resisted. His face dirty from the dusty embankment.

At the top, Jacob stumbled over his own feet. He laughed at his clumsiness. Standing on either side of him, Harry and David threw Jacob's arms over their shoulders and led him home.

They helped him home, to his house, not his parents. His mother would be awake. They didn't think he would sober up enough to climb stairs to his bedroom and his father would surely ridicule him.

In his drunken stupor, Jacob rambled on; he complained about his father, how he couldn't understand what he did to make his father hate him, how he couldn't wait to move into his own place.

The house was dark and dusty. In the parlor, blankets throw over the bits and pieces of furniture left by the former owners. They didn't bother lighting an oil lamp or a fire for warmth. They uncovered an old couch, found a cleaner quilted blanket in a storage chest, and covered their friend. Jacob fell asleep, or passed out, as soon as he laid down and as they closed the door, they heard the loud snores of their friend.

David and Harry walked down the path.

"It's barely nine o'clock," Harry said. "Wanna go to the tavern for a shot of good whiskey?"

"It is early. Let's go!"

They turned south on Poor Farm Road and headed towards Highland Park. In the distant, they caught sight of a large man briskly walking north across the fields. It was a quiet night and they could hear him whistling. The sounds faded as he disappeared over the horizon.

David and Harry hurried into the courthouse. They made their way to the second floor and slipped in the courtroom just before nine o'clock.

At exactly nine A.M. sharp, Judge Cooper exited his chambers and took his seat at this desk. As expected, the state rested. The defense began.

Hamill stood up. He called his first witness.

"The defense calls Harry Moore."

Harry stood up. He walked to the front of the courtroom and stopped at the witness stand. He placed his hand on the Bible and replied, "I do."

Harry sat down. Hammil stood up. He cleared his throat and began.

"Please state your name."

"Harry Moore."

"Harry, and your occupation?"

"I work at Des Moines Ice. I deliver ice."

"And your relationship with the defendant, Jacob Johansson?"

"Jacob and me go way back. Met in grade one. Been friends' ever since."

"Do you remember what happened the night of April 13, 1902? The night Jacob's siblings were murdered."

"Yeah, I do. We wus drinkin' hooch."

"We?"

"Me and my buddies. David, Eugene, and Jacob. Jacob drank too much night and um, he started to leave but he fell and um, we, I mean, David n' me figured we betta help him home. So, uh, we, uh, grabbed his arms and he didn't want' our help. He was bad shape and uh, we took him to his ol' farmhouse. The one he was fixin' up. There was ol' furniture, um, a sofa. It was covered with a cloth. Uh, we, uh, took it off an' uh, sat Jacob down. Jacob laid his head down an' passed out. Fell asleep."

"Thank you, Harry. What was Jacob doing when you left?"

"He wus uh-sleep."

"Could he have woken up?"

"Nah, a train couldn't wake him."

"Thank you. No further questions."

Hammil passed Jones on his way back to his seat.

"Good morning, Harry."

"G'morning," Harry mumbled.

"Was Jacob angry that night?"

"Yea, he was angry with his father."

"What about?"

"His father treated him poorly."

"And his brother, Timmy?"

"He said his father favored him."

"Favored him how?"

"Treated him better. Jacob did twice the work he did, but his father didn't care. Made a big fuss over Timmy all the time."

Claire's eyes saddened. Time after time, she intervened hoping to make life easier for Jacob, but Lukas never changed. She blamed herself.

Jones continued.

"How long did you stay at the farmhouse?"

"We left right away."

"And what time was that?"

"About nine o'clock."

"Do you know if Jacob woke up?"

"I don't think' he could have."

"That is not what I asked. I asked if you know if Jacob woke up."

"I wasn't there. We left."

"Is a possible that Jacob woke up?"

"I said I don't think' he would have. He wus in bad shape."

"Do you know if Jacob woke up? Yes or No?"

"Nah, I don't know if he woke up."

"Did you go home?"

"No, we went to the tavern in town."

"How long did you stay?"

"We had a whiskey and left."

Harry looked over at his friend. He hoped he said nothing that would hurt his case.

"Let me ask you this again. Do you know if Jacob woke up that night?"

"No, I do not. Cuz we left. But he was in bad shape. He, uh."

"Thank you. No further questions."

The bailiff instructed Harry to step down. Harry sauntered back to his seat next to David.

So, engrossed in his thoughts, David didn't notice his friend sitting down. He prepared for his testimony; remembering every detail of that night. He recalled walking Jacob home. He remembered walking to Highland Park's tavern. He remembered the darkness inside, a lone patron stood at one end of the long bar. The newspaper spread in front of him. David and Harry stood at the other end. Harry threw a dime down on the bar and raised two fingers up. He watched as the whiskey filled the glass. He remembered the aroma as he lifted the glass to his mouth and the warm feeling from his lips to the pit of his stomach. The aftertaste; bitter and soapy. The fire in the woodstove rose from the addition of fuel. He watched the fabric as it became engulfed in the flames.

Hammil stood up and announced, "Defense calls David Nicholson." Harry nudged David.

"What?"

"You are next," Harry whispered. "Get up there."

"David Nicholson," the bailiff boomed.

David sat up straighter when the bailiff called out his name. He stood up and walked to the witness stand.

"Do you swear to tell the truth, the whole truth and nothing but the truth, so help you God?"

"I do."

David took the seat. He glanced over towards his friend as Hammil made his way to the front of the courtroom.

"Please state your name."

"David Nicholson." Odd question, he thought.

"David, what is your occupation?"

"I'm a tenant farmer at the Murphy's farm."

"How long have you been there?"

"Since I was a kid. About ten. When my mama and papa passed."

"How long have you known Jacob?"

"Since grade school."

"Do you remember that night when his siblings were killed?"

"Yeah. Like Harry said, he drank a lot. He wus stumbling. We were 'afraid he would hurt himself. That's why we took him to his farmhouse. Didn't want to wake his father on account he wus tough on Jacob."

"Do you think Jacob could have done it? Killed his brother and sister?"

"Nah, Jacob wus mad at his father; not his brother, not like that. He had nuttin' against his sister. Nuttin'."

"Thank you, David," Hammil said. He turned towards the prosecutor and added, "Your witness."

The attorneys brushed shoulders as they passed each other. Neither man said a word.

Jones placed a paper on the podium in front of him. He had taken notes during the Harry and David's testimonies.

"David, both you and Harry said Jacob had drank too much, and you helped him home, am I right?"

"Yes, sir. That is what we said."

"And you both said he didn't wake up? Or you don't if he woke up because you left right away?"

"We left right away. He passed out."

"But you don't know if he woke up?"

"We don't know that."

"One more question. How can say he didn't do if you don't if he woke up?"

"Objection. This question has been asked and answered."

"Sustained. Mr. Jones, do you have any other questions for this witness?"

"Uh, uh, no, your honor."

"You may be excused," the judge said to David. As David walked past the prosecutor, he shot him an evil look. Quickly, he glanced towards Jacob; Jacob nodded.

David's thoughts returned to that fated night. He remembered sitting on his bed in his nightshirt. He stoked the fire that burned in the stove. The night air had chilled the room. He watched as the fire rose and engulfed the fabric. Within a few minutes, the shirt just a pile of ashes. David remembered slipping under the quilt. And minutes later, sound asleep.

The remaining part of the day filled with one witness after another. John testified that his brother had no ill feelings towards Timmy or Grace. Even during cross-examination, he didn't falter. Jones asked if Jacob knew about the changes to his father's will. John stayed strong. He replied, "Jacob had purchased his own farm and continued to help out his father every day despite knowledge of the changes."

The last to testify that afternoon was Emma's father.

"George Tucker," Hammil called out.

George stood up. His hat in his hand. He walked to the front of the courtroom.

"Do you swear to tell the truth, the whole truth and nothing but the truth so help you God."

"I do."

George sat down in the witness stand.

"Mr. Tucker, do you know the defendant?"

"Yes, I do."

"How long have you known the defendant?"

"His brother, John is married to my daughter, Emma. They married two years this summer. Jacob helped when they built their home."

"And recently, have you come to know him?"

"Jacob worked with me the past six months. I got to know the boy well. We worked side by side. He's a hard worker. Never complained. Just did what I asked of him."

"Did you talk to him?"

"When, uh, I finally talked him into takin' a break. We sat and talked. He told me about his farm. I was 'impressed. A young man buying his place at his age. That's unheard of."

"Thank you. No further questions."

Josiah Jones stood up.

"When you and the defendant talked, did you talk about his murder charge?"

"Yes sir. We did. He told me he didn't do it."

"And you believed him?"

"Yes. I did. He looked right into my eyes. I could tell he wus telling the truth. A man's eyes don't lie."

"You have known Jacob for a half a year and could tell he was telling you the truth. Is that correct?"

"I spent every day from dawn ta' dusk with that young man. He's a hard worker who gave me an honest day's work. I think of him like a son, yeah, he's like a son to me."

In the galley, Lukas groaned. The judge shot him a stern look.

Jones had no follow-up question. "No further questions."

The bailiff looked over at George Tucker and said, "You may step down."

Mr. Tucker step down and walked back to his seat. He nodded towards Jacob. *I'm like a son to him!* Jacob thought. He wished his own father felt that way.

Hamill stood up and called his next witness, "Adelaide Landers."

Adelaide stood up and walked to the front of the courtroom. She flashed the judge her signature smile. The judge smiled back.

After taking the oath, she sat down and folded her hands on her lap. She gazed over at Jacob.

"Can you state your name for the court?"

"Adelaide Landers."

"How do you know the defendant?"

"Jacob and I are courting."

"How long have you known Jacob?"

"Since grade school. And I am, was, friends with his sister. Grace. One of the victims."

"Have you and Jacob discussed these charges?"

"Yes sir. Many times, over the past six months."

Hammil asked Adelaide to describe Jacob's demeanor. She explained his fear. Fear he would be wrongfully convicted. How they discussed their future, their plans to wed, to start a family.

Whispers erupted across the courtroom.

I knew it! Chloe thought.

He hasn't asked for her hand in marriage. At least, not from me. Catherine wondered as she looked at her husband. She placed her small palm on William's forearm. William raised her right arm and patted her hand in reassurance.

"I never want to see him again," Lukas grumbled.

"Shh-shh," Claire whispered as she placed her index finger to her lips. "Do you want the judge to remove you?" I hope he and Adelaide have a happy life together.

The judge glared at the galley; they all hushed.

Hammil's last question, "Did you believe Jacob when he said he didn't commit the murders?"

CHAPTER 22

"Yes, I did. Jacob has never lied to me."

"Thank you," he replied as he turned towards the prosecutor. "Your witness."

Jones stood up; he cleared his throat and then asked, "How do you know he hasn't lied to you?"

"Well, he, uh, looks right at me."

"So, just a hunch?" Jones asked as he mimicked Hammil's comments from earlier testimony.

"No, not a hunch. I have known Jacob since I was five."

"Miss Landers. Were you also a key witness in your brother's trial?"

"I was a witness. I don't think I was a key witness."

"Did you not tell the courts you heard your brother come home?"

"I did. And I heard him."

"Objection!" Hammil called out. "This has no bearing on this trial."

"Your honor, I am trying to establish a pattern with the witness."

"Mr. Jones. Keep your questions to this trial only."

Jones looked down at his notes. He had nothing left to ask.

"No further questions."

Jones returned to his seat. He looked at the clock. With the noon hour approaching, the judge would call for a recess.

"We will recess until one o'clock," Judge Cooper announced as he slammed down his gavel. He stood up and walked out of the courtroom to his private office.

Jones looked at Culligan, "We have a lot of work over lunch."

Culligan stood. Jones stopped him, "I don't want to waste any time walking back to the office; we will work here." He tilted his head back towards the defendant, "after they leave."

The galley emptied fast. Everyone wanting to grab a quick meal to ensure a seat for the closing arguments.

Hammil walked back to his office. His confidence in winning this trial high.

Meanwhile, in front of the courthouse, Jacob and his siblings enjoyed the picnic lunch Adelaide had prepared.

John and Jacob each grabbed a chicken leg. "Hmmm," John said as he sunk his teeth into it. "If she cooks like this, you might get soft in the belly," he teased his brother. Jacob ignored him; instead his eyes on Adelaide as she talked and laughed with his sisters. Adelaide's sixth sense caused her to turn towards Jacob; the two locked eyes. She flashed him a smile but quickly turned to answer a question. Jacob's heart melted. He loved her so.

Adelaide lifted an apple pie out of the basket. She cut out a slice then handed the piece to Jacob. Adelaide continued serving the other siblings. John quickly ate then left to place a call to Emma. Hammil said he could use the telephone in his office.

John climbed the steps two at a time. He remembered that first day when he hired Hammil. He was pleased with this choice for his brother's attorney. Inside the attorney's office, he could hear Hammil's booming voice. He listened for a minute then realized the attorney was practicing his closing argument. Jacob hesitated before he knocked on his door.

Hammil stopped and opened the door.

"I have come to place a telephone call. To my wife, Emma."

"Sure, go ahead and make your call." Hammil pointed to the phone on his secretary's desk.

"I will be quick."

Hammil closed the door and restarted his practice; quieter this time.

John picked up the phone, turned the handle a few times to connect with a switchboard and informed the operator where to place his call.

Emma answered at once. She had just put the children down for a nap returning to clean the kitchen after two toddlers ate their lunch. John felt bad he hadn't been around to help. Emma understood; she knew he had to be there for his brother. John ended the call promising to hurry home as soon as court adjourned.

John left the attorney's office and returned to the courthouse. Out front, his siblings sat. Chloe and Anna Belle shared their babies' latest accomplishments. Anna Belle's daughter, Elizabeth scooted all over their house while baby Charlie tired Chloe with his constant desire to climb. John knew what they were going through. His own daughter, Lydia frustrated Emma as she crawled away any chance she could; their son, Timmy just happy to sit and play with his blocks.

The siblings continue to talk about their babies while Jacob and Adelaide watched and stole glances at each other. Hammil appeared from the other side of the building.

"Time to go back in," he informed the group.

"Wha, what happens now?" Chloe asked.

"Closing arguments; then the jury will deliberate."

"Will we know the final verdict today?" John asked.

"Not sure. It could be later this afternoon. Or tomorrow."

Adelaide sighed; her eyes full of tears. Jacob's heart ached for her. He wished he could take her away from here; escape the torment and move far, far away but as fugitives they would live in fear every day of their lives.

The courtroom filled in minutes. At exactly one o'clock the side door opened, and Judge Cooper exited.

"All rise," the bailiff called out.

When the judge had seated, everyone returned to their seat. Her turned towards the prosecutor and said, "You may begin your closing argument."

Jones stood up. He walked over to the podium and placed his papers in front of him.

"Ahem, ahem," he cleared his throat.

"Gentlemen of the jury. The past few days you have heard testimony about the anger the defendant, James Jacob Johansson had for his brother, Timmy. Anger that built up for years and exploded when the news his younger brother would inherit the farm. Exploding to where he wanted to hurt his father, he killed his brother and to hide this terrible crime, he killed his youngest sister too.

Gentlemen, the brutality of this crime is horrific. Jacob beat both siblings to death with a steel pipe. Hitting them repeatedly until they fell to the gravel road. They he continued beating them as they lay dying in the middle of the road; breaking their tiny bones, cracking their skulls, bruising their faces so bad their own mother couldn't recognize them. So badly beaten, the mortician couldn't hide their injuries.

And what did he do after bludgeoning them? He dragged their broken bodies to the ditches to die; a ditch filled with animal carcasses, mud, and water. Leaving brain matter, blood, and hair all over the road.

The death of his brother would guarantee Jacob would inherit the farm and double his farm size. A large monetary gain for him. Yes, the death of his brother would ensure he received the entire farm.

So, gentlemen of the jury, your task today is to return a guilty verdict and justice for sweet Gracie and little Timmy whose lives were cut short on that cool April night as they walked home from church.

Sentence this man, this evil man, to death. Let him hang from the highest tree. Let him live his final days in the darkness of a cell at Anamosa knowing that taking the lives of two innocent children is the reason for his own death. If only we could end his life twice once for each of the children."

Jones paused. He surveyed the jury. He felt his message strong; strong enough for a guilty verdict. He lowered his head and said "Thank you. With those last two words, he picked up his papers and walked back to the table.

Hammil took a deep breath as he waited for the judge's nod. Judge Cooper eyed Hammil.

Hammil stood up making his way to the podium. He laid his papers on the stand and step back. He had memorized his closing argument.

"Good afternoon, gentlemen. As citizens of the state of Iowa and members of the jury, you have the challenging task of determining this young man has a future. I ask you to look at the facts of the case. The evidence is weak. Based on hunches and not actual events. No one saw Jacob anywhere near that knoll. His friends testified he was drunk; so, drunk he couldn't walk. He had no blood on him or his clothing. The detective testified that there was blood splatter all over the gravel road. The killer would have been covered in blood, but his own mother said there were no bloodstains on his clothing and none of his clothing was missing following the murders.

The prosecutor wants you to believe Jacob killed his brother for profit. To inherit in father's farm but the largest part of the farm belongs to Claire Johansson and not Lukas. Claire had no intentions of willing her farm to just one child.

And I ask you, gentlemen, how many murderers ditch the weapon then retrieve it to turn over to the police? I can answer that question. Absolutely none! The detectives want you to believe Jacob was so conniving and intelligent to plan the attack but stupid; stupid to turn over the weapon after hiding it.

To the Johansson family, I'm sorry that this tragedy happened but putting Jacob to death for a murder he didn't commit is another tragedy. So, I ask you to return a not guilty verdict and let this young man and his bride to be start their life together."

Hammil held his arm out pointing towards Jacob. Behind him, Adelaide sat; her eyes pleaded with the jury.

Hammil added, "Thank you." He returned to his seat, put his arm around Jacob's shoulders and squeezed it. From behind, Jacob felt a light pat on his left shoulder; he reached up and covered Adelaide's small hand with his own.

Judge Cooper turned to the jury and said, "Please remember to base your verdict on the facts of the case only. Please deliberate as if you are deliberating for your own life." He turned to the bailiff and added, "You may lead them to the jury room."

Outside the courthouse, Adelaide sat on a bench across the road from the courthouse. She wore her favorite yellow dress with a fitted bodice and lace trim. Her long blonde hair swept up on both sides and secured with a carved oval barrette with pink orchids. A family heirloom handed down from her grandmother. At her feet, a multi-colored carpet bag held her belongings. Fear had the best of her. She tapped her fingers on the empty bench, bit her nails, and twisted her hair as she waited. Adelaide's nerves kept her from attending today.

Inside, a packed courtroom. Not a vacant seat. Besides the family, reporters from all the local newspapers sat with open pads in their hands. Sharpened pencils in their hands with a spare slipped over an ear. Absent for most of the trial, both Chloe and Anna Belle's husbands, Charles and Robert sat next to their wives. Chloe and Anna Belle held hands and prayed for Jacob's acquittal.

Catherine Landers McNally and her husband sat quietly. Catherine knew a guilty verdict would crush her daughter. She attended that day and hoped she wouldn't have to comfort her distraught daughter. William McNally had attended every day; he was more confident than his wife. As an attorney, he felt Hammil did his job and an acquittal possible, if not, probable.

On the other side, Claire folded her hands in prayer. Like her children across the aisle, she secretly hoped for a non-guilty verdict. She blamed herself for his trial. I should have said nothing to Pastor Griffin. It's all my fault Jacob is going through this, she thought as she stared straight ahead.

Lukas hoped they would sentence Jacob to death. Since the murder of his children, Lukas' faith diminished. He no longer attended any church service but even he prayed today. He prayed for a guilty verdict. He thought, I would put the rope around his neck. That murderer. If not death, he hoped he would rot in jail.

Pastor Griffin and Dr. Baker sat a few rows behind Claire and Lukas. Eliza Davis sat directly behind Claire ready to console her friend after they read the verdict. As Claire's closest friend, the two had many conversations since Jacob's arrest. She knew Claire regretted saying anything to her pastor.

Jacob sat next to Hamill; his heart raced' his palms sweaty. He turned to look behind him and noticed the empty seat next to his sisters. Adelaide noticeably absent but he understood. Adelaide expressed her apprehension earlier. She told Jacob she would wait outside. Their plans were in place. Jacob's sold his farm to Emma's brother. Part of the money, he used to pay his attorney fees; the other John held in the breast pocket of his jacket. If the jury delivered a not-guilty decision, they would leave at once to start their life away from Highland Park; away from the gossip and stares.

"All rise! The Honorable Judge Cooper residing," the bailiff called out. Both attorneys, Jacob, the jury, and the people in the galley all stood as the side door opened. Judge Cooper entered the room.

He took his seat at the front desk, picked up the gavel and slammed it down on the base, "Court is in session."

Everyone sat down.

"Have you reached a verdict?"

The foreman stood up and said, "We have, Your Honor."

"In regards to the State of Iowa versus James Jacob Johansson, what is your verdict?"

Outside, Adelaide continued to bite at her nails. Then she would hold the braids of her satchel tightly or twist her handkerchief in her hands. She heard the courtroom opened. Her heart sank as she watched several men run out. The reporters dashed to their newsroom to write the headline.

How long will it take? She thought to herself oblivious to the people who walked past her; eyeing the beautiful girl sitting on the bench. She daydreamed of her life with Jacob, their many babies, watching them grow and then suddenly, her eyes teared as she thought of him in jail or worse, hung for a crime she knew he didn't commit.

Thirty minutes later, her eyes reddened from crying, the door opened again. John and his sisters stepped outside. She tried to read their expressions. Her mama and stepfather followed them.

They look happy! Could it be? The door opened again, and Mr. Hammil exited the building. He shook John's and William's hands.

Adelaide cried; unsure whether tears of sadness or joy. And then, after what seemed like eternity, Jacob stepped outside.

Adelaide cried harder. Jacob and Mr. Hammil exchanged a few words as they shook hands. Mr. Hammil walked away leaving Jacob standing alone on the front step of the courtroom. He looked across the courthouse yard and saw Adelaide sitting on the bench. Their eyes locked.

Adelaide couldn't control herself. She stood up, lifted her skirt to free her feet and ran towards him. Jacob sprinted towards her.

They met halfway in the courtroom's middle yard. She jumped into arms as he lifted her in the air.

"You're free!" She cried out as she wrapped her arms around his neck.

"Yes. Not guilty. I'm free."

Behind them, Catherine and William stood. Catherine cried as William put his arm around her shoulders. Adelaide's siblings arrived just in time. David and Tom walked in front of Laura and her daughter, Mollie. Mollie skipped to keep up with the adults; a bouquet of coneflowers and clovers in her hand.

A short man carrying a bible approached them; a pastor from the church a few blocks away.

"Jacob Johansson?"

"Yes, that's me."

"Pastor Stevens," he said putting his hand out.

Jacob shook his hand and said, "Thank you for coming."

"Are you ready?"

"Not yet."

Jacob lowered Adelaide to the ground. He stood in front of Adelaide's mother and stepfather and cleared his throat before asking, "Mr. McNally, Mrs. McNally, may I have your permission to marry Adelaide?"

"Yes, you may," Catherine McNally replied. Her husband, William nodded in agreement.

Jacob turned around. In front of Adelaide, he got down on one knee, took her hands and in front of his siblings and her parents, he asked, "Adelaide Landers, will you please marry me and make me the happiest man in the world?"

Adelaide covered her mouth with her hands, she thought she

would cry, her voice cracked as she said, "Yes. I will."

"Right now," Jacob said as he stood up. Her pointed at the pastor standing nearby.

"Yes, yes," she said as tears flowed down her cheeks. Jacob wrapped his arms around her.

"Please don't cry or I will think you don't want to marry me."

Adelaide released herself from his grip and looked up at him with her tear-stained cheeks, she smiled.

"Much better. Now let's go get married."

Mollie ran up to her aunt, handed her the bouquet and said, "For you." Adelaide took the flowers, leaned down and kissed her niece on the top of her head. "Thank you. They are beautiful!"

Mollie beamed with pride. She had helped her mama pick them earlier that day.

Jacob and Adelaide stood before the pastor. John next to Jacob; Adelaide's sister Laura beside her.

The rest of the group stood behind them. Chloe and Charles, Anna Belle and Robert and Catherine and William formed a half circle behind them. William lifted Mollie and put her on his shoulders, so she could watch her aunt marry. David and Harry stood in the back.

The Pastor began the ceremony. Under a bright red tree, he began.

"James Jacob, do you take Adelaide Catherine to be your

lawfully wedded wife? Do you promise love her, comfort her, honor and keep her, in sickness and in health? And forsaking all others, keep only to her as long as you both shall live?"

Jacob looked in to Adelaide's eyes, smiled and said, "I will."

"Adelaide Catherine, do you take James Jacob to be your lawfully wedded husband? Will you obey him and serve him, love, honor and keep him, in sickness and in health? And forsaking all other, keep only to him as long as you both shall live?"

"I will," Adelaide nodded and replied. Her eyes filled with tears. One escaped the corner of her eye. Jacob lovingly wipe it away.

"Repeat after me. I, James, take you Adelaide to be my wife," the pastor paused for Jacob.

"To have and to hold, from this day forward, for better or for worse, for richer, for poorer, in sickness and in health." Another pause.

"To love and to cherish until death do us part. With all my worldly good, I thee endow."

Jacob repeated the statement perfectly.

The Pastor looked at Adelaide.

"I, Adelaide, take you Jacob to be my husband."

A teary-eyed Adelaide slowly repeated the words, her voice cracked as she tried not to cry.

"To have and to hold, from this day forward, for better or for worse, for richer, for poorer, in sickness and in health."

By now, the tears were running down her face; she lifted her hand to wipe away the tears before she started.

"To love and to obey until death do us part."

Adelaide took a deep breath. She had practiced these lines since she was a young girl.

She flashed Jacob a smile; that smile that melted his heart, and said, "to love and to obey until death do us part."

Adelaide handed her bouquet to Laura. Jacob took the gold band from John and slipped it on Adelaide's ring finger as he said, "With this ring, I thee wed."

The Pastor opened his bible and said a quick prayer before he added, "I now pronounce you, man and wife."

Jacob and Adelaide smiled at each other.

"You may kiss the bride," the pastor said to Jacob.

Jacob lifted Adelaide's chin with his hand and lowered his head. She felt his breath as he pressed his lips against hers. She grabbed his forearms to keep from falling over.

Everyone cried and cheered at the same time.

Meanwhile, Claire and Lukas had walked outside. Lukas still furious at the recent verdict; mumbled "Jacob is dead to me. Dead to me." Claire ignored him and looked over at the group standing at the corner of the yard. She meandered and from a distance watched her son marry. The woman he was meant to be with for the rest of his life. She could see his face. He smiled at his bride. She could see the love in his eyes. For the first time in a long time, he looked happy. And that pleased Claire.

Jacob looked up and saw his mother. She smiled at him and he smiled back. She knew he would leave town now. She hoped they would return someday.

Lukas glanced over but when he realized who it was, he tightened his mouth and looked straight ahead. He mumbled something Claire couldn't understand but knew it wasn't anything nice.

After the ceremony, the group said their goodbyes. Catherine hugged her daughter as she fought back the tears. Adelaide had told her their plans to leave town.

Catherine loosened her grip and whispered in Adelaide's ear. "Be happy, my darling daughter. Love your husband with all your heart. Stay safe. And please write when you settle in."

"I will, mama. We will be close enough for you to visit."

Adelaide hugged her new sisters-in-law. "I wish you didn't have to go so far away," Chloe said.

"When things settle down, we may be back."

Anna Belle repeated Chloe's sentiments. Her thoughts drifted on the school play yard. She remembered how Adelaide watched Jacob play ball and told everyone she would marry him someday.

Once the goodbyes said and promises to write vowed, Jacob picked up his bride and carried her to his wagon. In the back, his belongings. David retrieved Adelaide's bag from across the street and carried to the wagon.

"Thank you for everything, David," Jacob said.

"Safe travels."

Catherine ran to the wagon. She and Adelaide hugged one more time. Catherine wiped away her tears. William joined them. Only married to Catherine a few months, he had grown fond of her children, especially Adelaide. He hugged Adelaide and told her, "If you need anything, anything at all." She nodded. Since her father died when she was just a baby, William was the closest thing to a father for her.

He shook Jacob's hand and made him promise to keep Adelaide safe.

"I promise, Mr. McNally."

"William, please call me William. We are family now."

Catherine and Adelaide held each other for a long time. Catherine wiped away her tears. She looked into her daughter's eyes and hoped she would see her again. William pried the two apart. They only had a few hours of daylight left and knew they should leave soon.

"As soon as you're settled, please write. We will send the rest of your things. I love you, my darling Adelaide."

"Oh, mama, I will. I promise you. Jacob says when all this is behind us, we can come back."

Catherine hugged her new son-in-law. "Promise me you will take care of my daughter, you will love her for the rest of your life. And you will come back and bring your family."

"I promise you."

After all the hugs and tears were over, Jacob lifted Adelaide into the front of the wagon and climbed in next to her.

"Ready, Mrs. Johansson," he said as he squeezed her hand.

"I'm ready, husband."

And with a snap of the reins, they pulled away. Adelaide looked back and waved.

The others watched as they disappeared down the road. Everyone left when they were out of sight. Except for Catherine and William. She knew in her heart they needed to move away to make a fresh start, but it didn't make it any easier. She felt William's hand on her shoulder; she reached up to hold it. Her eyes filled with tears.

CHAPTER 23

David and Harry stood watching their friend leave. They made their way to the trolley station.

"Do you think Jacob will ever come back to Des Moines?"

"Maybe, when everyone has forgotten it. In a few years, no one will remember."

"I hope he and Adelaide are happy."

"Let's cut out the small talk."

David stopped walking. He looked around to see if anyone was close enough to hear him.

"We both know what we did. We take it to our grave. You understand, Harry, our graves."

"Our grave. No one will ever know what happened," Harry paused then added, "that night."

The two men shook hands and continued to the trolley station.

ABOUT THE AUTHOR

Originally from the East Coast, Julie Metros now lives in a suburb of Des Moines, IA (close to the murder scene) with her two pets, Cooper a rambunctious cocker spaniel puppy and Maggie, her bossy tabby cat. She has one son, Daniel.

Julie welcomes interviews, speaking engagements, educational interactions, book club meetings, etc. (Both in person and remotely.) She may be available on short notice. Please contact her at jam923m@msn.com, check out her Facebook page, Julie Metros, Author, or visit her author page at authorcentral.Amazon.com.

Made in the USA
Middletown, DE
21 May 2019